FELIX DASHWOOD AND THE MUTATING

LUKE TEMPLE

Collect all the 'Felix Dashwood' series:

☐ Felix Dashwood and the Traitor's Treasure

☑ Felix Dashwood and the Mutating Mansion

☐ Felix Dashwood and the Traitor's Revenge

Collect the 'Ghost Island' series:

☐ Ghost Post

☐ Doorway To Danger

☐ The Ghost Lord Returns

About the Author

Luke Temple was born on Halloween, 1988. When Luke was a child, he didn't enjoy reading, he was terrible at spelling and found writing hard work. Yet today he's an author! When not writing, Luke spends most of his time visiting schools and bringing his stories to life with the children he meets.

To find out more about Luke and his books, including fascinating facts, fun videos, downloads and hidden secrets, visit his website:

 www.luketemple.co.uk

FELIX DASHWOOD AND THE MUTATING MANSION

To everyone at
Parnwell Primary!

Luke

June 2016.

LUKE TEMPLE

Gull Rock Publications

Dedicated to the two Cyrils:
one fictional, one real,
both no longer with us.

With thanks to Jessica Chiba, Catherine Coe, Gareth Collinson, Mike
and Barbara Temple, Kieran Burling and the Highfield Hall Jury

www.luketemple.co.uk

First published in Great Britain by Gull Rock Publications

The paper used in the printing of this book has been made from wood
grown in managed, sustainable forests.

ISBN: 978-0-9572952-3-0

Printed and bound by CPI Group (UK) Ltd, Croydon, CR0 4YY

A catalogue record of this book is available from the British Library

Thistlewick Island

Explore an interactive map of Thistlewick
at: **www.luketemple.co.uk/map.html**

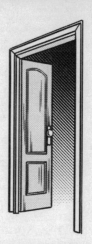

1

The Old Abandoned Mansion

Felix heaved another load of newspapers onto the shelf at Thistlewick Island Newsagent's. She had given up doing it neatly and just dropped them down into a scattered pile. She was fed up.

It was all her mum's fault. She'd gone to a Thistlewick Island council meeting half an hour ago and had asked Felix to sort out all the newspapers for her. Ask was probably the wrong word – threaten was more like it. And on the first day of the summer holidays too.

Felix wished she was with her friends, Caspar and Drift. They could be having some kind of adventure now, even if it was unlikely to be as exciting as the one they'd had a month ago, when they'd been hunting treasure. They'd ended up battling an evil, ghostly pirate crew and also discovered that their head teacher was actually an escaped criminal called Tristan Traiton, who'd been trying to steal the treasure himself.

She looked back at the shelf and rolled her eyes. She

would have to neaten the newspapers up. If she didn't, Mum would just make her do it all again.

As she straightened a stack of *The Chronicles of Thistlewick*, she glanced at the front page. There was a large photo of an old building under the headline, 'MURKHILL MANSION TO BE DEMOLISHED, FINALLY'.

Felix wasn't usually interested in reading newspapers, but something about the photo made her curious – maybe it was because Murkhill Mansion looked so run-down. She focused on the first paragraph of writing.

Murkhill Mansion, on Forest Lane, was, for a few years, a mysterious place. Little is now known about the mansion's last occupants, except that they were the Summercroft family, who lived there until 1965. They had rented it from an eccentric English inventor, Mr Blaze. Then, one night in July 1965, the family went missing. What's more, several others who were alleged to have visited the mansion in the days after the family's disappearance are themselves rumoured to have vanished. Maybe they all moved away from Thistlewick, or perhaps it was something more sinister.

For a while, Murkhill Mansion was feared and people believed stories about curses and evil goings-on. Now, over fifty years later, the mansion is simply an old ruin. The council have wanted to knock the place down for many years, but until very recently it was still under the ownership of Mr Blaze.

'Mr Blaze was an odd chap', Mayor Merryweather told this newspaper. 'He had not visited his mansion on Thistlewick for fifty years, and failed to find new tenants to rent it. I have sent him countless letters requesting that the mansion is demolished – it is an unsightly place to look at – but he has always flatly refused'.

However, Mr Blaze passed away in England last month. With no heir listed in his will, the ownership of Murkhill Mansion has transferred back to the Thistlewick council.

'Plans are now in place to have the mansion demolished, and we hope that this will take place very soon', said Mayor Merryweather.

When the demolition happens, the mayor is hoping to turn it into a big event and invite everyone on Thistlewick to watch. To find out more, turn to page 15.

Felix looked up as a thought struck her. Murkhill Mansion was an abandoned, run-down place that hadn't been lived in for years. There were rumours of curses and evil goings-on.

She couldn't stay at the newsagent's now – not when there was something so interesting to investigate.

***

Felix placed her hand on the rusty gate and carefully pushed. It gave way and she walked through into a badly overgrown garden. Caspar followed close behind and Felix could tell he was already getting nervous. He looked far too neat and tidy, wearing a perfectly ironed T-shirt and spotless shorts.

Drift leapt over the garden gate and landed next to them. Like Felix, he had on his usual scruffy jeans and a T-shirt caked in mud and sand.

'Won't your mum be annoyed that you've left the newsagent's?' asked Caspar.

'I'll worry about that later. Anyway, I deserve a lunch break.'

'You'd only been working for half an hour!'

Felix shrugged.

'Well, I have to go and help my dad down at the harbour this afternoon, but I've got all morning,' said Drift. 'So what's the plan?'

'Let's have a look around.'

Felix walked cautiously through tall weeds and over roots, which ran along the broken stone path like dead snakes.

The building loomed tall in front of them now, far bigger than any of the other houses on Thistlewick. If anything, it looked more of a wreck than the photo in the paper.

'Why have I never noticed this place before?' Felix wondered.

'I don't think we've ever been around here, have we?' replied Caspar.

'That's true.'

They were on a high cliff as far east as it was possible to go on Thistlewick. All that surrounded the building was the forest on one side and the sea behind it. The buildings back in the main part of Thistlewick were small specks on the horizon.

Halfway up the garden path, Felix found a sign. She cleared the weeds from around it and could just make out some cracked, swirly writing: 'Welcome to Murkhill Mansion'.

'This is definitely the place!'

She looked up at the building again. The walls were grey where the paint had peeled off and had thick ivy growing up them, there were cracks running through the bricks, windows were smashed, half of one of the chimneys was missing and the roof looked like it might collapse at any minute.

Caspar glanced at the mansion, eyebrows raised. 'I am *not* going in there.'

'Last month we were trapped in a cave, about to be killed by a group of ghost pirates. Why are you scared of this place?' asked Drift.

Felix smiled at her friends and walked up to the large oak front door, which was sheltered in a porch. She took hold of the knocker and hit it three times against the door. The loud noise echoed through the mansion.

'If there's anyone inside, they'll definitely hear that,' said Drift.

Felix waited several minutes, but there was no sound of movement.

Caspar shuffled uncomfortably. 'Can we go now?'

As Felix stared at the door, she noticed the doorknob standing out. She had never seen one like it before – it had a smiling, golden face on it. Unlike the rest of the mansion, the doorknob was far from dirty and shone brightly at her. This made Felix's mind up.

She reached out and turned it.

The door swung open.

Felix stepped inside and Drift soon joined her.

She looked back out into the garden. 'Come on, Caspar!'

He stared up at the crumbling walls, then sighed and stepped forwards. 'Fine, I suppose someone has to keep an eye on you. But I am not staying in here for long.'

Felix grinned. She knew Caspar didn't like adventures as much as her, but she was really glad to have him there. He had nearly had to move away to England earlier in the year after his mum lost her job. Then, when they won the treasure, they used it to buy Caspar and his mum a house, so they could stay on Thistlewick.

As Felix's eyes began to adjust to the dim light she saw a vast, tall hallway with a white marble staircase in the middle. She couldn't help feeling a bit disappointed. She didn't quite know what she'd expected – perhaps loads of golden statues leading to a gigantic throne at the top of the stairs; or maybe something spookier like a gruesome ghost chamber filled with skeletons. But the entrance hall just felt empty.

'This stinks,' said Drift.

'We can't give up yet.'

'No, I mean it literally stinks. Where's that smell coming from?'

Felix sniffed and a mixture of rot and old cabbage ran up her nose. She screwed it up and walked towards the staircase, her footsteps echoing on the stone floor.

As she placed a foot on the first step she felt something brush against her.

She looked behind her, but in the darkness she couldn't see anyone there. There was another movement and she turned quickly around. A dark figure stood in front of her.

Felix slowly stepped back, her heart thudding in her chest. The figure had a giant head with devil's horns coming out of it.

Just then, a beam of light flickered across the entrance hall. Felix let out a sigh of relief. It was just a statue – a marble carving of a large eagle, perched on the staircase banister.

Felix turned to where the light had come from. Drift was at the left of the entrance hall, standing in the doorway to another room, from which the light emanated.

'Hey, Caspar,' he called over. 'Need the toilet?'

'Why would I need the toilet?'

'There's one here. Don't want you to wet yourself.'

Caspar glared at Drift. He always teased him.

Felix looked past them and another door caught her attention. It had intricate markings carved around its edge, with swirls curling in various symmetrical patterns. There was a word cut into its wood at the centre, in the same artistic lettering as the sign in the garden: 'Library'.

'Caspar, look.'

He followed her gaze. 'That doesn't sound too scary. Is the door—?'

Before Caspar finished his sentence, Felix had shot over to the door and twisted the handle. The door glided open with ease.

Inside, two of the walls were completely covered from floor to ceiling with bookshelves, a third contained a large fireplace, and the wall opposite Felix had a tall window which gave a magnificent view of the sea and the sky.

'A proper library,' Caspar said, mouth wide in awe.

Felix smiled. 'Bet you're glad you came into Murkhill Mansion now.'

Caspar went straight over to one of the bookshelves.

Felix looked back to Drift. 'You coming in?'

Drift shook his head. 'A library doesn't sound that interesting. I'm going to see what's behind some of these other doors.'

Felix turned back and began to search around the library, keen to find anything that might tell her more about the mansion and why it was abandoned.

On the mantelpiece above the fireplace she spied a collection of silver photo frames. The smallest one, circular with a thin crack running through the glass, contained a black and white photo of a girl who looked about the same age as Felix. She had shoulder-length hair and a freckly face. The photo was faded, but the girl's eyes and smile seemed alive.

The photo behind it was bigger, in a rectangular frame, and showed the same girl with a man and a woman. In this photo, the girl was in a wheelchair and, although she was smiling, she didn't seem as happy.

'This must be the family that used to live here.'

'Felix, come and look at this,' Caspar called over.

She turned away from the mantelpiece and found Caspar staring at one of the bookcases, a curious look on his face.

'You really do like books, don't you?'

'Look at them, though.'

It didn't take Felix long to realise what Caspar was getting at. 'They all have white covers.'

'Except that one.' He pointed to a book with a bright red cover.

'Why's it different to the others?'

'I suppose whoever put it there must want us to look at it.'

'Go on then, pull it out.'

Caspar took hold of the book and slid it off the shelf. It was in perfect condition except for the cover, which had some thick vertical scratches down it. Felix counted them: eight. Under the scratches, in golden lettering, was written, 'Amelie's Diary'.

The book fell open to the first page and Felix and Caspar began to read.

2

July 1ˢᵗ 1965

Dear diary,

Hello! My name is Amelie Summercroft and I live in Murkhill Mansion on Thistlewick Island. Ok, so that is a bit of a boring way to start, but this is my first ever diary entry and I couldn't think of anything better.

Today was my 10th birthday. I couldn't have cake, because that would make me too sick, but all the presents made up for it.

Mum and Dad's present was you – my first diary. What should I use you for? There would be no point in me writing down what happens each day, because not many exciting things happen in my life. It's kind of difficult to have adventures when you're stuck in bed. Mum and Dad think I should use you to write stories. They are always telling me that I have a big imagination. Mum also thinks that if I write down all the nightmares I have, it might stop them. Dr Ralph said I should write about it too, but I really don't want to think about that.

I know a diary doesn't sound like a big present, but it's Ok. Mum and Dad have to spend a lot of money on me. They haven't said that to me, but I know that all the medical equipment in my room is expensive.

I also got some drawing pencils from Uncle Ferdinand and a sketchpad from Aunt Cariola. Other than the fact this stinks of Aunty Cariola's horrible perfume, it is a perfect present – I love drawing.

Another thing I love is reading. If you can't have adventures of your own, the next best thing is to read about them. Most of my other presents were books, and I am almost looking forward to lying in this bed all day now that I have all these adventures to go on.

The best present of all, though, was a surprise one. It was wrapped in shiny red paper and the label on it read: 'Dear Amelie, I hope this helps you to make your dreams come true. From Mr Blaze'. I didn't even know who Mr Blaze was until Dad told me he is the person we are renting this mansion from. Murkhill Mansion is far too big for the three of us, but apparently Mr Blaze insisted we take it. He lives in England and we have never met him, so Mum and Dad were really surprised he even knew it was my birthday.

Dad helped me to unwrap the shiny red paper and I pulled out a rag toy. It is about twenty centimetres tall and wears a long black coat, like a magician's cloak. Its face is the best bit, though – like a golden, smiling theatre mask. I turned it round to show Mum and she said it gave her the creeps. But I love it! How did Mr Blaze know that my favourite thing in the world is theatre? I have always dreamed of writing my own plays and acting. (Not that that's ever going to happen now.) I decided to call my rag toy Shakespeare, after the most famous playwright in the world.

The only thing that could have made my birthday even better today was if I had seen my classmates from school. I really miss them – even Bartley, who always annoyed me.

I haven't talked to my toys since I was about five, but this evening I found myself telling Shakespeare how much I wished all my friends could have been here today. But none of them came. It was just me and Shakespeare, who smiled at me as I told him all about them. Of course he smiled – he's a toy, that's all he can do. He's sitting at the end of my bed now. I've just told him that I am writing about him. A 10-year-old girl talking to her toy. It's a bit sad, isn't it?

Still, I do love his smile.

3

Changing Rooms

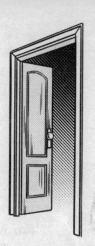

'I feel sorry for Amelie, not having any of her friends there on her birthday,' said Felix.

'It sounds like she wasn't allowed out of bed,' said Caspar. 'I wonder why?'

'That must be so boring.' Felix tried to imagine that happening to her and just couldn't. It was bad enough when Mum grounded her in the house. But to be trapped in bed all day must be awful. 'No wonder Amelie started talking to her toy. When did she write that diary entry?'

Caspar looked at the first page again. 'July 1st 1965.'

Felix remembered the newspaper article. 'So Amelie and her parents disappeared soon after she wrote that.'

'What happened to them?'

'Don't know – the newspaper just said they mysteriously disappeared. Come on, let's go and show Drift the diary.'

Felix walked over to the library door and opened it. She blinked – it took her a few seconds to realise what she was seeing. In front of her was a thin, narrow kitchen. Frowning, she closed the door, waited a moment and opened it again.

It was definitely a kitchen, with work surfaces along two walls and an ancient cooker and fridge at the far end.

Felix closed the door, turned back and scanned the library.

'What's up?' asked Caspar.

'I'm not dreaming it – we definitely came into the library through this door, didn't we?'

Caspar nodded. 'There aren't any other doors in the library. What are you getting at?'

'Open the door.'

Frowning, Caspar did so. Felix watched as he took two steps backwards and turned to face her, eyes wide. 'That doesn't make any sense.'

Felix stepped into the kitchen and called, 'Drift! Drift, can you hear me?'

There was no reply.

Felix walked along the kitchen until she came to a window. It gave a view of the weed-covered garden, and behind that the towering trees of the forest.

'We must be in a different part of the mansion.'

'How did we…?' Caspar's voice trailed off.

'I don't know, but let's try this next door.'

They walked to the door next to the fridge at the far end of the kitchen. It opened out into…

'A bedroom?'

Felix quickly took in her surroundings – a large double bed, two oak wardrobes and a dressing table to the right. She went straight over to the window on the left. The view out of it was similar to the one out of the kitchen window, except from higher up – Felix was looking down on the garden from above.

'We're on a different level, Caspar. It looks like this bedroom is above the kitchen.'

He joined her at the window and shook his head. 'But how can we have gone through a door in the kitchen and ended up in the room above it?'

Felix looked around the bedroom. 'We need to find Drift.'

She ran over to a door next to the bed, calling out Drift's name. The next room was a living room, with three plush armchairs facing a tiny square box that Felix realised was an old-fashioned TV. She opened another door and found herself in a toilet – the same toilet that Drift had discovered in the entrance hall, with a long metal chain dangling down from the cistern above it. There were no other doors in there, so she stepped back out into the living room.

'Over here,' said Caspar, beckoning Felix to a door on the other side of the room. It creaked open to reveal a small corridor with light green walls, leading to a narrow staircase.

'Brilliant. If we go down those stairs it should take us to the ground floor,' said Felix.

At the bottom of the staircase, Felix felt something sticky on her face. She went to brush it off and felt her hand cutting through thick spiders' webs. She pushed through them and in the dim light realised she was surrounded by cardboard boxes in a triangular-shaped room. Felix looked up – wooden beams stretched across the ceiling.

'We're in the loft!' Caspar realised.

'So the stairs going down took us *up* to the loft? This is crazy. How exactly do we get out of here? The stairs have disappeared!'

'There must be a loft hatch somewhere.'

Caspar squeezed himself around the boxes and Felix began searching too, careful not to bang her head on the wooden beams.

'Aha!' Caspar bent down over a square of light and felt around. 'If I can just find the…'

Something clicked and the loft hatch flew open, sending Caspar catapulting downwards head first.

Felix ran over to the hole and saw Caspar in a heap on the floor below. She carefully manoeuvred herself through the hatch, landing next to him on the floor.

'Drift!'

He was sitting in what looked like a grand, golden throne. He wore a shining silver crown that matched it.

'Well, you two certainly know how to make an entrance. How did you end up up there?'

'You won't believe it…' said Felix, taking in their

surroundings. The walls were made of rough, giant pieces of stone, more like a castle than a mansion. In fact, behind the throne there was a tapestry on the wall of knights on horses fighting in a medieval battle. 'Hang on. Where are we?'

'Pretty cool, huh? This crown was just sitting on the throne, waiting for me.' Drift grinned. 'Now, why don't you kiss your king's feet?'

Caspar pushed himself up. 'Where did you find this room?'

'I got here through a door in the entrance hall.'

'Go and have a look back out of that door again, Drift,' said Felix.

'Why? Did you find something out there?'

'Just open the door.'

Drift went over, turned the handle, looked out and reacted in exactly the same way that Felix had in the library. His eyes widened and he quickly shut the door and opened it again.

'Woah! What on earth…?'

'All the rooms are muddled up,' Felix explained.

Drift stepped through the door and Felix heard him say, 'Cool!'

Felix and Caspar joined him. This room had a red rug down the middle leading to the window with a view of the sea, and the walls were covered in paintings, like a small art gallery. They were mainly of children playing with dolls, climbing trees and riding horses – or was it all the same child, just at different ages? One painting in the middle of them all stood out – a portrait of a tall, thin man. He had black, greased-back hair, and his facial expression was hard to read. It was almost a smile, but there was sadness behind it. Felix read the name written on the painting's frame: Mr Blaze.

'That's the man who Amelie's parents rented Murkhill Mansion from,' said Caspar.

'Who's Amelie?' asked Drift.

'We found her diary in the library. She lived here with her parents until they all mysteriously disappeared,' explained Felix. 'But anyway, how did we end up here? This room-changing thing is weird. Me and Caspar have been going all over the place.'

'We can't find our way back to the entrance hall – which means we can't get out of the mansion,' Caspar added.

Drift's eyes landed on the window. 'Sure we can. We'll just have to climb out through there.'

'I am not doing that,' said Caspar.

Drift shrugged. 'You can stay here then.' He walked over to the window and tried the latch, but it wouldn't budge. 'It's locked. Well, I guess one more won't make a difference.'

'One more what?' asked Felix.

'Broken window – we can smash our way out.'

'Drift, you—'

Before Caspar had a chance to protest, Drift elbowed

the window and the glass splintered into a thousand tiny pieces.

Drift stuck his head out through the hole. 'Easy. The garden's right outside this window. We can climb straight out and— Aaahhh!'

He jumped away from the window as the glass that had smashed flew up off the floor and floated in the air like many tiny daggers pointing straight at Drift. Then it shot into the window frame and started to stick itself back together, like a see-through jigsaw puzzle.

The repaired glass glowed bright white ... and suddenly a face pushed out of it. Felix gasped and staggered backwards. The face was looking straight at her, its eyes shining menacingly and with a wide, evil grin. It was like a demonic version of the golden face on the doorknob of Murkhill Mansion.

There was a blinding flash of light. When Felix's eyes had recovered she saw the window was as good as new. It didn't look at all like Drift had just smashed through it.

'Did you see that face?' asked Felix.

Caspar nodded and said in a shaky voice, 'That was freaky. And how did the window repair itself like that?'

Even Drift looked shocked, his usual cool exterior replaced by a tense frown. 'So much for finding an easy way out.'

'Any other bright ideas, Drift?' asked Caspar.

Drift glared at him and puffed out his chest.

Sensing her friends were about to start arguing, Felix

said, 'Come on, there aren't any other doors in here. We'd better head back into that castle room.'

But when she opened the door, the castle room was no longer behind it. Her eyes fell on something even weirder.

July 2nd 1965

Dear diary,

I had a nightmare last night about school. I always loved school, except for geography with our head teacher, Mr Thrasher. He was really strict and, although I never usually got told off, I still found him terrifying. But the worst thing was that Mr Thrasher made me sit next to Bartley.

In my nightmare we were doing a geography test. About halfway through it, I noticed Bartley was looking over my shoulder at my answers. I looked at his paper – his answers were the same as mine. He had been copying me.

I whispered, 'Stop cheating, or I'll tell Mr Thrasher.'

Bartley grinned, but then I saw that he wasn't looking at me – he was looking behind me.

I turned around and Mr Thrasher was there,

towering over me, his fiery eyes burning into mine.

'This is a test! Why are you talking?' he roared.

'I … it was…'

'She's copying my answers, sir,' Bartley interrupted. 'Look, she's written the same as me.'

I tried to protest, but Mr Thrasher grabbed hold of my paper, glanced at it, then ripped it to pieces. I felt warm tears running down my face and realised everyone was now staring at me.

'Why are you crying?' Mr Thrasher boomed. 'I am appalled at you, girl. I will not tolerate cheating! You will spend the rest of the lesson writing out the following lines: I am a cheat. Cheating is wrong. If I ever cheat again, I will be shut in Mr Thrasher's cupboard for the whole day.'

I tried to stop myself crying but it was no good. He was like a huge red dragon spitting fire at me – then he really did turn into a dragon, with razor-sharp teeth. I looked into his bloodthirsty eyes as his snake-like head hovered over me.

I tried to remember the technique Mum had taught me for getting rid of my nightmares. I had to tell myself I was in charge of my imagination and turn my mind into a castle, which I was the queen of. I had to imagine that in the castle's dungeons there were prison cells with thick iron bars. Then, as queen, I could order the bad thing in my nightmare to be locked away in the dungeons.

I tried this with the dragon Mr Thrasher. I imagined

him being chained up and dragged into the dungeon. Behind the bars, he thrashed his dragon tail around. But he couldn't break them - the bars were too strong. I allowed myself to smile slightly and my nightmare started to fade.

But then the dragon Mr Thrasher turned back to me and his eyes glowed bright red. He opened his dragon mouth and a ball of fire shot straight at me.

I woke up with a scream. It was morning - bright light beamed through the curtains.

I turned over and saw a plate full of food, a glass of water and my medicine on the bedside cabinet. Mum and Dad must have left it there while I was sleeping. That was odd, because usually they wait until I'm awake to give me my breakfast, help me take my medicine and have a chat.

The morning seemed to drag on and there was still no sign of Mum or Dad. Maybe they'd had to go out. But wouldn't they have come in and told me?

My nightmare made me think back to all the bad times at school. I sat my Shakespeare rag toy on my lap and told him about the day I was playing snakes and ladders with my best friend, Elfie. There was a giant snakes and ladders board painted onto the playground and we played using really big counters and a dice the size of a cardboard box.

I rolled the dice and it landed on a six. Just as I went to move my counter, Bartley came up and grabbed hold of it. He started running around the playground with it,

25

sticking his tongue out at me. I chased after him. Round and round the playground we went and everyone else stopped their games and watched.

Then my shoelace came undone. I tripped and fell straight into a puddle. I wiped the dirt from my face and looked up, and saw Bartley standing there, grinning down. Right then I wished that one of the snakes from the board would come and eat Bartley up.

I stood up and looked around the playground. Everyone else was staring at me, laughing. Even Elfie couldn't stop a giggle.

Maybe none of my classmates like me. Maybe that's why none of them came on my birthday.

I felt tears welling up in my eyes. I hugged Shakespeare and held him out in front of me.

'You're my only friend right now. Look at you, with that smile. You'll always be happy listening to me. I wish I had more friends like you.'

I must have fallen asleep in the afternoon. When I woke I had a fresh plate of food and what looked like two more presents sitting on my bedside cabinet. Had I missed Mum and Dad coming in again?

I leant over and picked up the presents, both wrapped in emerald green paper with no label. I felt them – they were squishy. It took me a while to open them, because my fingers aren't very strong now. As I peeled the paper away from the first one, I recognised a familiar face – a golden mask with a big smile, just like Shakespeare's. In fact, it was identical to Shakespeare – a rag toy with a long black coat. The second present was exactly the same.

I decided to call them Romeo and Juliet, after characters from one of Shakespeare's plays. I even made them name badges out of paper, so I could tell them apart.

'Now you've got friends,' I told my Shakespeare, sitting them down next to him.

This evening I decided to teach Shakespeare, Romeo and Juliet how to play snakes and ladders. The only problem was that my snakes and ladders board was somewhere in the bottom of my wardrobe and I couldn't get out of bed to find it.

But I had an idea. I used my new sketchpad and pencils to draw the game, and told my rag toys about throwing the dice and moving your counter up ladders and down snakes.

Reading all this back, it feels like I have had a busy day. I still don't know where Mum and Dad have got to, though.

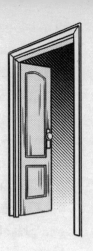

5

Snakes and Ladders

Stretching out in front of Felix was the biggest snakes and ladders board she had ever seen. The windowless room was probably the largest they had been in so far, but the board took up most of the floor. It was lit by spotlights from above and divided into red and yellow squares, numbered from 1 to 100. Scattered around the board were various full-sized ladders and a number of green snakes – painted on, but they looked like they might slither off the board at any moment.

Caspar froze solid. 'Those snakes almost look real!'

'Wow!' said Drift. 'Look at the size of them. That snake over there must be about five times the size of me.'

He wandered over to the board to take a closer look.

Felix frowned at her friend. 'You don't seem that bothered by all of this, Drift. A giant snakes and ladders board, rooms changing around…'

Drift shrugged. 'It's just a trick, isn't it? Some sort of

optical illusion, like at a theme park.'

He stepped onto the snakes and ladders board.

'That's interesting,' Caspar muttered.

'What is?' Felix turned to see him studying Amelie's diary.

'In the second diary entry, Amelie talks about drawing a snakes and ladders board.'

Caspar showed Felix the diary.

'She also talked about turning her mind into a castle,' Caspar explained. 'That room we found Drift in looked like the inside of a castle, and now we've found a snakes and ladders board. That's a bit of a coincidence.'

'Amelie's parents probably built them for her,' Felix suggested.

'Maybe, but that doesn't explain how the rooms are all muddled up.'

'Like Drift said, it's an optical illusion.' Felix wasn't sure if she really believed this, but what other explanation was there for the strange things that had happened?

'Er … guys,' said Drift. 'I'm stuck.'

Felix turned to see him standing on square 1 of the board.

'I can't move.'

'Don't be an idiot, Drift,' said Caspar.

'I mean it. Look.'

Drift lifted his leg up and tried to move it onto the floor outside the board. But as soon as his foot reached the edge of the board, it just stopped, as if there were an invisible wall around him. Drift screwed up his eyes in concentration and kicked outwards again, but it didn't help.

For the first time, a flicker of panic appeared on his face.

'Try moving along the board to square two,' said Felix.

Drift moved his foot, but as soon as it reached the line that divided square 1 from square 2, it shot backwards.

'I think,' Caspar said slowly, 'that you're the counter. You have to play the game.'

'Look – there's the dice.' Felix had noticed it sitting next to the board. It was black with white spots and to scale with the board – almost the size of a sheep.

'If Drift is the counter, maybe we have to roll the dice for him to move,' Caspar suggested.

Felix walked over to the dice. Bending down, she gripped the bottom of the shiny dice with her fingers and levered it up. She didn't get very far before her fingers gave way.

'It's too heavy. I need your help, Caspar.'

Caspar came over and pressed his hands against the side of the dice.

'Can you two hurry up, please? I'm getting bored now,' said Drift.

'Ready?' said Felix. 'One, two, three!'

Felix and Caspar pushed the dice as hard as they could. It swayed forwards and rolled straight along the floor to the other end of the room.

'A three,' Felix announced. 'Try moving now, Drift.'

Drift tentatively put out his foot – this time it kept going. He stepped over to square 2 and then onto square 3, then 4. When he tried moving onto square 5, though, something stopped him.

'It's definitely linked to the numbers on the dice then,' said Felix.

'So the only way you can get off the board is to reach square 100 and win the game,' said Caspar.

Drift rolled his eyes. 'Great! The last time I played snakes and ladders it took me an hour to get to the end. Hurry up and roll the dice again.'

Felix and Caspar positioned themselves behind it.

'One, two, three!' called Felix.

The dice rolled back along the floor.

'Five,' Caspar called out.

Drift moved along 5 squares.

The next roll produced a 4 and Drift walked along to square 13.

'Hey, there's a ladder on this square. I wonder if it'll let me climb— Whoa!'

Felix gasped as Drift's feet were whipped from under him. He fell down onto the ladder and was dragged up it by some invisible force to square 33.

He laughed as he stood back up. 'I want to do that again!'

Felix looked at the squares that came after 33. 'Right,

we need to roll anything but a 2 – that snake on 35 would take you all the way back to square 11.'

Felix and Caspar braced themselves and heaved the dice again. It rocketed along and bounced off the wall opposite, eventually coming to land on … a 2.

Drift jumped over to 35 and stared down at the head of the snake. 'Does this mean I have to slide back down?'

He jolted backwards. It took Felix a second to realise why – the snake's head was lifting itself up off the board and moving towards Drift.

'OK, that's not cool,' said Drift.

The snake no longer looked painted. It was 3D and very alive – just like a real, giant snake. Felix tensed as the snake hissed at Drift, its tongue flickering. She watched, wide-eyed, as it started to wrap itself around his left leg. He gasped and tried to move away but it was no good – he was trapped within the square as the snake slithered up him.

Felix looked at Caspar. 'What can we do?'

'Roll the dice again!' he suggested through deep, panicky breaths.

They rolled the dice away from them. It landed on a 1.

'Try moving one square to your left, Drift,' said Caspar. 'Drift?'

But when they turned back to him, Drift was almost completely covered by the snake, its scaly skin glinting in the spotlights. Only his head was now visible and his

eyes were wide with fear. He tried to call out but no sound came.

Felix ran towards the board, but Caspar grabbed hold of her arm. 'No, Felix, you can't! You'll only get trapped in the board too.'

'We have to help Drift!'

But Drift's head had disappeared inside the snake's grip. It was too late. The snake hissed at Felix and Casper, and its head started to glow red. It changed shape, contorting into a mask-like face, with a wide grin – just like the face that had appeared in the smashed window.

Felix looked on, open-mouthed, as the grin widened further. Then, with a thud, the snake collapsed back into the board, once more stretched out from square 35 to square 11, a motionless painting, its head that of a snake again.

'Where ... where's Drift?' asked Felix.

'He's disappeared!' Caspar mouthed.

July 3rd 1965

Dear diary,

Food, drink and medicine were left on my bedside cabinet again this morning, but still no sign of Mum and Dad. I tried calling out to them a few times, but they never came. It's not as if they would have heard me anyway – I can't shout like I used to.

The problem with lying in bed all day with not much to do is that you worry about things more than most people. Before, I was happy and not much really bothered me. But now I worry about everything. About whether Mum and Dad can really afford to rent this mansion and pay for my treatment. About what my friends all think of me and why they don't come over. About <u>it</u>. Even about the spider I accidently squashed when I put my glass of water down on the bedside cabinet yesterday. What happens to it when it dies? What will happen to me? The spider's body is still lying there under the glass.

Most of all, though, I am worrying about why Mum and Dad haven't come in to see me when I'm awake. Maybe I've done something to upset them, although I can't think what.

At least I have Shakespeare and Romeo and Juliet. Whenever I look at them, sitting at the end of my bed, I seem to forget all of my worries and their happiness spreads over me. I know they're not actually happy – they're just bits of cloth and stuffing. But they look like they are.

I tried reading a book this morning. It was about a girl who went on an adventure in a forest. She climbed a tree and found a nest of golden eggs. I had to stop reading halfway through because it made me jealous. I stared out of my bedroom window at the Forest of Shadows. I should have done so much more when I was able to walk. I should have climbed trees and swum in the sea and explored caves. Now I will never be able to do any of those things.

Then I got annoyed at myself for being selfish. I have had a life full of friends and happiness, and my parents have always made sure I have felt loved. I couldn't ask for any more that that. Not all children are so lucky. Even though I can't climb trees, why shouldn't a girl in a story be allowed to do so?

To keep myself busy I picked up my sketchpad. I spent the afternoon drawing Murkhill Mansion over and over again, imagining all the different ways I would build a mansion if I was an architect. I made it look like a doll's house and in each drawing I moved the rooms around. In one picture, I placed the kitchen right next to a bedroom, in another the toilet was in a cupboard in the living room. In my final drawing I turned Murkhill Mansion into my mind castle and drew the dragon Mr Thrasher locked up in the dungeon.

I've just looked at the calendar on my wall. Dr Ralph is meant to be coming to see me later this afternoon. I like Dr Ralph. He's not like the horrible doctors at the hospital who talk really seriously and use scary words that I don't understand. Last time he was here he juggled the needles before giving me my injections and made my pills magically appear from behind my ear! Knowing that I will see him later has cheered me up.

***

It is now the evening. I thought I heard someone outside my door earlier and tried calling out, but there was no reply. It was probably just my imagination playing tricks on me.

Dr Ralph didn't come. And there's still no sign of Mum or Dad.

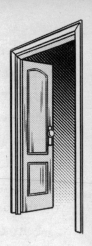

7

Dr Ralph's Note

'Pinch me, Caspar.'

'What?'

'This is too weird. That can't have just happened to Drift. I think I'm dreaming. Pinch me and hopefully I'll wake up.'

Caspar grabbed a bit of skin on her arm and squeezed it.

'Ow! OK, it's not a dream.'

Caspar tried pinching himself for good measure. 'No, this is definitely happening.'

'So where has Drift gone?'

'Felix, look at Amelie's diary, there are nine scratches on it.'

'No, there are eight. I counted them earlier.'

'So did I. There's a new scratch.'

He held out the diary. Caspar was right – a ninth scratch was freshly dug into it.

'What does that mean?'

'I think everything that's going on must have something to do with this diary. Amelie writes about a castle, we find a room like a castle. She writes about a giant snakes and ladders board, we find one. It's like her imagination is coming true.' Caspar's eyebrows rose and he flicked the diary back open. 'Amelie says that she wanted one of her classmates to be eaten by a snake. Do you think that's what happened to Drift?'

Felix didn't know what to think, but what Caspar had said worried her. 'No, it can't be. He'll be in the mansion somewhere.'

She went back to the door that led to the room of paintings.

'Where are you going?'

'To find Drift. Come on, Caspar – but keep reading the diary. There might be more clues in there about what's going on.'

But when she opened the door Felix found herself back in the kitchen.

'Drift!' she called, running along the hard stone floor.

Caspar shuffled along behind her, his eyes on the pages of Amelie's diary. 'Amelie is talking about drawing Murkhill Mansion and mixing all the rooms up.'

Felix shot through the door at the other end of the kitchen and stumbled into another room that looked like it belonged in a castle. This one was round, with narrow slits for windows and longbows hung up on the wall.

'Drift!'

Casper caught up. 'She even drew Murkhill Mansion like it was a castle. I was right – whatever she wrote down here is coming true.'

'Anything else? Anything that gives us a clue about where Drift might have gone?'

Felix moved left, to a thin oak door. Pinned to it was a piece of paper.

'Not really,' said Caspar. 'Now she's talking about a doctor who's meant to be coming to see her but doesn't show up.'

'Dr Ralph?' asked Felix.

'Er … yes. How did you know that?'

'Because Dr Ralph wrote this note.' Felix pointed to the piece of paper on the door. She read out the wispy writing. '"Saturday 3rd July 1965, 4 p.m. My name is Dr Ralph. I came to Murkhill Mansion to see my patient, little Amelie Summercroft, but I think I am going mad. I have been stuck here for several hours now. There is no sign of anyone else and the rooms keep changing. I have found myself entering the same room on multiple occasions, but each time through a different door. This cannot be happening. I have decided to write these notes and pin them to the doors, so I can keep track of which door leads where. Through this door is a pantry."'

'So Dr Ralph did come to see Amelie,' said Caspar.

'But he got lost, like us. Shall we see if we can follow his notes?'

Caspar nodded. 'It might help us find Drift.'

Felix opened the door and, as Dr Ralph's note suggested, she found herself in a pantry, with various cupboards and a table piled up with tins and bottles.

The next door had two notes pinned to it, both with the same wispy handwriting. Felix took one, Caspar the other.

'Mine's from 4.03 p.m. on 3rd July,' said Felix. 'It says, "When I arrived at the mansion no one answered the door. I took it upon myself to enter. I have lost count of the number of rooms I have been through now, but I can't find anyone. Where are Mr and Mrs Summercroft? This door leads to some sort of dungeon."'

'Mine is from 8 a.m. on 4th July.' Caspar frowned at the note. 'Felix, that means he was trapped here for more than a day!'

'What does the note say?'

'"I am tired, I am thirsty, my vision is blurred, and now I have gone round in circles and find myself in the same room again. I must not lose focus. I must find Amelie. Without proper medical attention, she will not survive. I have looked through this door again. I must have got it wrong yesterday – it does not lead to a dungeon, it leads to a conservatory."'

Felix opened the door and light flooded in from the sun outside. Through the glass walls of the conservatory, Felix saw what must be the back garden of Murkhill Mansion – just as overgrown as the front and surrounded by a low fence – and in the distance the deep blue sea.

'Look, there are doors to the garden.' Caspar pointed. 'It's a way out of the mansion!'

'Let's have a look. We can always try to get back to this conservatory again when we've found Drift.'

Felix went over to the glass door and pushed down on the handle. The door opened out and a blast of cold air hit Felix as she stepped forwards. She looked down and saw her foot hovering over thin air, where a moment ago there had been garden. The sea, which had been the other side of the garden fence, was now directly below her – at least fifty metres below, with sharp rocks jutting dangerously out of it. The door had opened out right onto the edge of the cliff!

She quickly pulled her foot back in and slammed the door shut. 'We can't get out here!'

She backed away and joined Caspar.

'Where now?'

'The door on the other side of the conservatory, I guess.'

On this door they saw several notes pinned – all in different handwriting.

'Other people have got lost here, too,' Caspar realised. He squinted at some small handwriting. '"Archie Addlestrop, 8th February 1971".'

'"Enoch Shipman, 20th November 1993",' Felix read. 'He says he's been stuck here for five days!'

Felix looked at one note, which seemed to have been written by a child. '"Elfie Smallwood, 7th July 1965" –

that's just a few days after Dr Ralph's notes.'

'She was one of Amelie's friends from school, I think,' said Caspar.

In total there were notes from seven people pinned to the door, including Dr Ralph.

'What happened to all these people?' Felix wondered.

'Maybe they got stuck here for good and … and…' Caspar started shaking.

Felix knew what he was getting at, but she couldn't let Caspar's worries get to her. She looked him straight in the eyes. 'Like Dr Ralph said, we can't lose focus. We have to keep going. We have to find Drift.'

She opened the door and stepped through into a short corridor. At the other end was a white door with a sign attached to it. The sign was bordered by lots of colourful flowers and read 'Amelie's Room'.

8

July 4th 1965

Dear diary,

I have been trying to figure out the answer to a riddle. Dad asked me it when he woke me up on my birthday two days ago. He always asks me riddles on my birthday, like these ones:

<u>Riddle on my sixth birthday</u>: Who can jump higher than a mountain?

<u>Riddle on my seventh birthday</u>: Four fingers and a thumb yet flesh and bone I have none, what am I?

<u>Riddle on my eighth birthday</u>: Mary's father has 4 daughters: Martha, Maggie and Mandy. What is the last daughter's name?

<u>Riddle on my ninth birthday</u>: I am the beginning of everything, the end of time and space, the beginning of every end, and the end of every place. What am I?

I am usually really good at riddles and all these didn't take me long to solve:

On my sixth birthday, I knew the answer in five minutes: Anyone, because mountains can't jump!

On my seventh birthday, I knew the answer in three minutes: A glove!

On my eighth birthday, it took me twenty minutes to get the answer: Mary! (Why did it take me so long? The answer is obvious!)

On my ninth birthday, it took me six minutes: The letter 'e'!

Dad used to tell me I am so good at riddles that when I grow up I should have a job inventing riddle books. But that will never happen now.

I always took the riddles into school the day after my birthday and Elfie and I asked Bartley them. He was useless and it made him really mad when we wouldn't tell him the answers.

The riddle Dad asked me two days ago is the toughest

one I have ever heard, though. Apparently it is one that his dad, my granddad, asked him on his tenth birthday. It took Dad three days to figure it out. He said he would tell me the answer if I didn't get it within three days. Well, the time's up now and he isn't here to tell me. Where have my parents gone? That is a bigger mystery than the riddle.

I am beginning to think that something bad has happened to them. What if they have had an accident somewhere else in the mansion?

Sorry if that last sentence is a bit smudged. I couldn't help crying when I thought about something bad happening to Mum and Dad. But then I looked at Shakespeare and Romeo and Juliet and my worries disappeared. They reminded me about my riddle.

Here it is. I still haven't solved it, but maybe if I write it down that will help:

'You are trapped in a building and there are two identical doors in front of you. One door will lead you to safety, but behind the other is a ferocious lion that hasn't been fed for a week. Guarding each door is a knight, and the knights know which door leads where. The knight standing in front of one door always speaks the truth, but the knight standing in front of the other door always speaks lies. There is no way of telling which door is which, or which knight is the liar and which is the truth-teller. You are only allowed one question, which you can only ask one of the knights. Can you figure out which door will lead you to safety?'

Writing it down hasn't helped, but I am going to try drawing the doors and getting my rag toys to help me.

**

I drew two identical doors on two pieces of paper and propped them up at the end of my bed. Then I stood Romeo and Juliet in front of the doors. Shakespeare sat with me and I asked him the riddle – but we still couldn't work it out.

Now I'm worried about going to sleep tonight and having nightmares about being eaten by hungry lions!

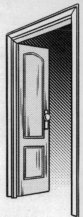

9

Two Doors

Felix read Dr Ralph's note on Amelie's bedroom door.

'"July 4th, 11 p.m. I have found her!" That's all it says, Caspar.'

Caspar walked silently up to the door.

'Shall we go in?' Felix looked at her friend and he gave her the faintest of nods.

She twisted the doorknob and the door swung open.

Felix sighed. 'Of course not.'

The room in front of them wasn't Amelie's bedroom. The door had opened to reveal a small, square castle chamber with thick stone walls. Felix and Caspar walked in and heard the door shut itself behind them.

Felix froze. In front of them were two medieval knights in full suits of armour, each guarding a thick wooden door.

'Hello?' she said warily.

They didn't reply. Felix walked up to the suit of armour on the left. After what had already happened in this mansion, anything could be inside it. Holding her breath, she quickly lifted up the armour's visor.

She breathed again. 'It's OK, Caspar, these are just empty suits.'

'There's no point carrying on, is there?' came a small voice.

Felix turned to see Caspar slumped down against the opposite wall. 'What's the matter?'

'We're going from room to room and not getting anywhere. We'll just end up going round in circles, like Dr Ralph did.'

'But he might have got out…'

'Him and all those other people who had been trapped here for days? It's hopeless. We're not going to find Drift and we're not going to get out of here.'

Felix went and sat down next to him. 'One way we can guarantee not finding Drift, or getting out of here, is if we just give up now. We have to keep going.'

Caspar's head dropped.

'Can I have a look at Amelie's diary?' asked Felix.

Without looking at her, Caspar passed it over. If everything that was going on had something to do with Amelie's diary, there must be a clue in it somewhere. Flicking through the entries they had already read, Felix came to the next one, dated July 4th 1965.

Poor Amelie – her parents still hadn't come in to see her. Maybe they had got lost in the mansion, like Dr Ralph and the other people.

Amelie was talking about riddles, none of which Felix could solve. But she thought they might cheer Caspar up.

'Hey, Caspar, what has four fingers and a thumb but no flesh or bones?'

He sniffed loudly. 'A glove. I've heard that one before.'

'OK, how about—'

'I'm not in the mood, Felix.'

'Fine.'

She continued to read through the entry, and stopped suddenly. She looked up at the two identical knights, guarding the two identical doors in front of her.

'Caspar…' she began. 'We're in a riddle right now.'

'What do you mean?'

'Amelie's written about this in her diary.' She showed it to Caspar and he stared at the two knights.

'There wouldn't actually be a lion behind one of those doors, would there?' he asked.

'Well, if a snake can rise up out of a board game and make Drift disappear, then, yes, I think there probably is a lion behind one of those doors. But which one?'

Caspar took the diary and studied it.

Felix walked up to one of the knights to take a closer look again. Its silver armour shone brightly.

'Don't ask them anything, Felix!' Caspar said quickly. 'If we really are in a riddle, then we can only ask one question to one of them to find the safe door.'

Felix turned back to Caspar. 'So, any idea how to solve the riddle?'

He shook his head.

'Well, there's no point in wasting our time on it. Let's go back.'

She walked over to the door they'd come through and opened it.

'Oh no!'

A solid brick wall stood in front of her. There was no way past it.

'Caspar, we can't get out this way!' Felix slowly closed the door as the realisation struck her like a lead weight in her stomach. 'Our only way out is through one of the doors that the suits of armour are guarding.'

Caspar rolled his head back against the wall and clenched his fists. 'Oh, great. We're trapped in the riddle, like Drift was trapped in the snakes and ladders game.'

'Yes, so we'll have to focus. Right. Behind one of those doors is a lion, behind the other is safety. One of the knights is a liar, the other one tells the truth. And we can only ask one of them one question to find out which is the safe door?'

'Yes.'

'Then we just need to figure out which of the knights is a liar,' Felix said confidently. 'So … if we asked one of them "Are you a liar?"'

'Then they'd both say no,' said Caspar.

'Why?'

'Because the liar would lie and tell you he wasn't the liar.'

'OK, so what if we asked a really obvious question, like "How many knights are there in this room?" If we ask the truth-teller, he'll say two, but if we ask the liar, he'll say a different number. Then we'll know which knight is which.'

'True. But we'll have used up our one question. We won't then be able to ask the truth-teller which is the safe door.'

'Oh … I hate riddles. This is impossible!'

'Let me think for a minute.' Caspar closed his eyes and rubbed his temples with his hands.

Felix stared at the knights, willing them to tell her which was the safe door. The suits of armour just stared ahead, unmoving and expressionless.

'Ah!' Caspar looked up, his eyes brighter. 'We can't find out which is the liar without using up our one question. The only way to find out which is the safe door is to ask which is the safe door.'

'Right…'

'But we have to ask one of the knights that question without knowing whether he's the truth-teller or the liar.'

'Uh-huh,' said Felix, just about following.

'So we need to ask a question that will make both of them give the same answer. But what?'

'I don't know. You're the brainbox. Wouldn't they always give different answers?'

'Hmmm…' Caspar closed his eyes again.

While she waited, Felix thought about Amelie. How could her imagination be turning into reality? How could it be causing all of this to happen?

'Got it!' Caspar stood up and ran over to the knight on the left-hand side. 'Which door would the *other* knight say is the door that leads to safety?'

The knight suddenly sprang into life. Caspar jumped back as it stepped towards him.

'Caspar!' Felix leaped up to protect him from the knight.

'It's alright, Felix, look.'

The knight didn't attack but raised an arm and pointed towards the door the other knight was standing behind. Then it froze in that position.

'So … you've worked it out?' asked Felix. 'We just go through the door that knight is pointing at?'

'No. The safe door is the other one, the one on the left.'

'OK… What?'

Caspar smiled and walked towards the door the knight hadn't pointed at. Felix watched him, surprised. For Caspar, he was being strangely confident. Why wasn't he worried that he might have chosen the door with the lion behind it?

He grabbed hold of the handle and said, 'Come on.'

Caspar opened the door to reveal … a flight of stairs leading downwards.

As if to confirm they had made the correct decision, a deep, loud rumble of a roar came from behind the other door, making the knights' armour rattle.

'Yep, you definitely chose the right door. Excellent work, Caspar!'

They went through and Felix closed the door behind them.

'So how did you know which guard was which?'

'I didn't,' said Caspar, 'and I still don't.'

'You mean you just guessed?'

'No. The question I asked meant that it didn't matter which knight I asked. They would both have pointed to the unsafe door – the one with the lion behind it. That's why we went through the other door.'

'Right,' said Felix, not understanding at all.

She looked at Caspar. He was still smiling – at least solving the riddle had cheered him up. Then she saw what he was looking at. The staircase in front of them was the white, marble one that led to the entrance hall, and there below them was the front door of Murkhill Mansion.

'That door really did lead us to safety. It's taken us to the exit,' said Caspar.

'That's if the front door still leads to the garden outside.' Felix remembered what happened when she'd opened the conservatory door.

'Let's find out.'

They ran down the stairs and over to the front door.

As Felix turned the handle and opened it, blinding sunlight spread through the entrance hall. Outside she saw bushes and weeds and the front gate of Murkhill Mansion.

'Fresh air!' Caspar sighed and stepped out into the garden.

Felix walked out too and felt a gentle breeze blowing through her hair. It was a relief to be out of the mansion. She looked up at the outside of it. It still looked just like the old, run-down place they had first come across that morning. There was no sign of the weird things that had happened inside it.

'I think Drift might have been right,' said Caspar.

'What do you mean?'

'Well, it might all be based on Amelie's imagination, but this mansion could just be a strange sort of theme park that her parents built. A mix of a maze and games and riddles where the challenge is to find your way back to the entrance hall.'

'You're saying that we've completed the challenge?'

Caspar nodded. 'And maybe Dr Ralph and the other people who left notes completed it too.'

'But what about Drift? Where is he?'

Caspar thought for a minute. 'Maybe he was just thrown out of the mansion.'

'So if you lose you get chucked out, but if you complete the challenge you get to walk out through the front door, like we have? That's a pretty rubbish prize.'

'I don't know. It's just an idea.'

Felix looked at her watch. 'Well, it's four o'clock. Drift said he had to go and help his dad out this afternoon, so if he *was* thrown out of Murkhill Mansion, he'll probably be at the harbour.'

10

July 5th 1965

Mum and Dad looked up at Murkhill Mansion from the beach below.

'Do you think Amelie will be alright, all alone in there?' asked Dad.

'We have done all we can for her,' said Mum. 'It is best we leave her now.'

'Are you sure?'

'We are doing the right thing.'

'Where shall we go?'

'England. We will start a new life there. We can raise a new child. A healthy child.'

Mum and Dad stepped into the small, wooden boat. They had packed all their worldly possessions into it. Their clothes and books, Mum's prized orchids and Dad's collection of model cars. They had decided to take only one photo of Amelie with them, as a small reminder of the daughter they were leaving behind.

Dad fired up the boat's engine and it sped off into the night, bouncing over waves under the moonlit sky, on its way to England.

***

Dear diary,

And that's when I woke up screaming! For a horrible minute I thought it was all true. It was still dark outside, but I wanted to run to my window to see if I could spot a boat out at sea. I even tried to lift myself out of bed, but it was no use – I had no strength in me, and anyway, I am attached to all the machines by wires.

I told myself to calm down. To breathe. It was only a nightmare. Mum and Dad would never just abandon me like that.

But what if they have? What if they have left me here?

I didn't get much sleep for the rest of the night and by the morning I felt really ill. I went from hot to cold to hot again and my whole body was shaking. I tipped out my bottle of pills into my hand. There were only four left, and I am meant to take two each day. That means I only had two days of pills left.

I swallowed one of the pills and looked at Shakespeare, hoping he would cheer me up.

That's when I saw the object on the bed next to me.

Wrapped in purple paper, it was another squishy present. It took me a whole half an hour to open, I was so weak. But I guessed what was inside: another theatre-mask rag toy, identical to the others. Where are these toys coming from? They can't all be presents from Mr Blaze.

I placed the new toy next to Shakespeare and Romeo and Juliet. I decided to call him Hamlet, after another of Shakespeare's famous characters.

All four of them looked at me with their golden smiles. I forgot all my worries and felt happy again.

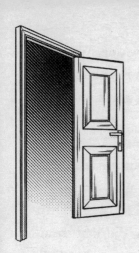
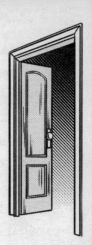

11

Rag Toys

Felix and Caspar stopped off at Drift's house on the way down to the harbour, but no one was in.

They carried on towards the sea, which was calm, with lots of small waves lapping against the shoreline and sparkling in the late afternoon sunlight. Only one boat was moored up in the harbour, gently rocking in the water. Beside it, Drift's dad was untangling a net, his bushy eyebrows furrowed in concentration.

'I'll go down and ask Oakley if Drift is around,' said Felix.

She left Caspar sitting on a bench, reading more of Amelie's diary. Felix climbed down the steps, past the rickety, old harbour hut and over to the jetty.

Oakley was so busy trying to unpick a particularly tight knot that he didn't notice Felix. She coughed.

'Oh, hello, Felix,' said Oakley, looking up. 'You haven't seen Drift, have you?'

'I thought he was meant to be helping you, Mr Castle.'

'Meant to be, yes, but he hasn't shown up. With the day as nice as it is, I thought he might have forgotten all about helping his old dad and be messing about with you.'

'So you haven't seen Drift all afternoon?'

'No. He's probably still lazing around in bed, the rascal.'

Felix looked anxiously back up at Caspar. If Drift wasn't at home or down at the harbour, did that mean they were wrong and he was still stuck inside Murkhill Mansion? Caspar wasn't looking her way, though – he had his head in Amelie's diary.

Just then, Mayor Merryweather appeared, clambering down the harbour steps. He was a round man with a grand white moustache that had a life of its own. As he strode towards them, his moustache formed into a smile.

'Hello, Felix, hello, Oakley. I hope you don't mind me interrupting. I just wanted to confirm everything for tomorrow morning, Oakley.'

'Did the council meeting go well this morning?' the fisherman asked. He stopped working on his net and pulled an orange out of his pocket.

'Oh, yes. Everyone has agreed my plans. The demolition of Murkhill Mansion will go ahead, beginning tomorrow morning. It will be a grand event, I am sure, and everyone is invited to watch!'

'Tomorrow morning?' Felix asked in a voice slightly louder than she'd intended.

'Indeed,' the mayor replied. 'And about time. That building has been a blot on our landscape for too long.'

'What time will the machinery arrive?' asked Oakley, peeling his orange.

'The chap from the demolition firm said that their ship would be here at first light tomorrow morning. I am told the ship is a fair size, carrying bulldozers, wrecking balls, a crane – the lot. Where would it be best for them to land?'

Oakley scratched his head. 'Burnt Tree Bay, I reckon. It's nice and wide and there are no cliffs round there, so the beach leads straight onto the main island.'

'I will advise them accordingly.'

'I'll make sure I'm at the bay at first light to guide them in.'

'Perfect!' Mayor Merryweather exclaimed. 'See you tomorrow then.'

With a twirl of his moustache and a wink at Felix, the mayor walked away from the harbour.

'Well, I never. Bulldozers and wrecking balls. Tomorrow should be an exciting day.' Oakley turned back to Felix. 'Are you OK, Felix? You're looking very pale.'

'Oh … yes,' said Felix.

'Have you had lunch yet? You look like you might faint.'

'No.'

'Then have one of my oranges. In fact, take a couple,'

said Oakley, pulling two large oranges out of his pocket.

Felix took them. Although she hadn't eaten since breakfast this morning, she didn't feel hungry – she was too worried for that. 'Thank you. I've … I've got to go.'

She walked back over to the steps.

'If you see Drift, tell him to get himself down here before the sun sets,' Oakley called after her. 'I've got some fish he can gut – he likes doing that.'

Felix nodded.

'Drift's not here,' she said as she reached Caspar, throwing one of the oranges into his lap. 'I think he's still in Murkhill Mansion – and it's being demolished first thing tomorrow morning!'

Caspar looked up from Amelie's diary, his eyes dark and serious. 'Yes, I think Drift is still trapped, and I think Dr Ralph got trapped inside fifty years ago, and Amelie's parents too. There's something odd going on.'

Felix sat down next to him and peeled her orange. 'What?'

'We know that something is taking the things Amelie imagined and making them real. It muddled up all the rooms in Murkhill Mansion when she did that in her drawings; it created an actual giant snakes and ladders board and a real-life riddle. But there's something else strange. Going through her diary, I've just realised – the first time Amelie says her parents didn't come into her room was on 2nd July, and two theatre-mask rag toys appeared that day. Then, Dr Ralph got lost in Murkhill

Mansion. The last note we found from him was at 11 p.m. on 4th July. On 5th July Amelie says another rag toy appeared in her bedroom.'

Felix bit into her orange, and only realised as she swallowed the juicy pieces how much she'd needed to eat. 'So every time someone disappeared in the mansion, one of those toys turned up on Amelie's bed?'

'Yes. I've double-checked Amelie's diary and it all fits together. Somehow it's all connected to those toys. I just don't know how, or what's causing it.'

Felix stood up. 'Then we have to go back to Murkhill Mansion. We have to figure out what's causing all this and what's happened to Drift. And we have to do it before the place is demolished tomorrow!'

July 6th 1965

Dear diary,

This is not a nightmare! This is real!

Three huge, ugly men walked into my room this morning and started unplugging me from all the machines. The men were dressed in black with thick, tree-trunk arms. I tried to kick out, but they held me down. I screamed and shouted for Mum and Dad to help me, but my voice was so weak. The men lifted me onto a stretcher.

I couldn't even grab hold of my rag toys before the men carried me out of my room.

They took me outside. I'd been indoors for three weeks. If I hadn't been so scared, I might have enjoyed the breeze and sunlight. But it felt like the wind was tearing into me, the sun blinding me.

As the men carried me away from Murkhill Mansion, I started shaking. I felt sick from the movement of the stretcher and closed my eyes...

I must have fallen asleep, because the next time I opened my eyes, I was in a room where everything was white.

Two men with greased-back hair and a woman with a tight bun stared down at me and scribbled on their clipboards. I had no doubt they were evil doctors.

It was the first time I had been in a hospital since I found out about _it_ and I was terrified.

'What am I doing here? Where are my mum and dad?' I asked.

'You will not being seeing your parents again, I am afraid,' said the female doctor.

'They sent you to us,' said one of the male doctors.

'So that we can use you in our experiments!' said the other.

Their eyes flashed evilly and they walked out of the room.

Since then I have been locked in here on my own, connected up to new, bigger machines. I don't even have Shakespeare here to comfort me.

All I have is you, my diary.

What are the doctors going to do to me?

***

Dear diary,

Ok, so it was a nightmare. My brain just tricked me. I thought it was real because at the start I was writing in my diary about everything happening. But how could I have had my diary with me in hospital? That's when I realised I was dreaming.

These nightmares are getting too clever, though. I never used to have nightmares. They all started when I found out about _it_, after those horrible men took me to the hospital for the first time and my life changed forever. Now Mum and Dad aren't here to help me control the nightmares, they're getting worse. My mind castle obviously isn't working - I need to find a better way to get rid of them.

I've spent most of today reading non-fiction books. One of the books I got for my birthday is about true but strange and funny deaths. I thought I would be scared about death, but I don't think I am, not any more anyway. I'm scared about the pain that _it_ might cause as _it_ gets worse, but not death. I've never thought about death being funny before, though.

My favourite death is Aeschylus's (I still don't know how to pronounce that), a Greek actor who died in 456 BC. He was acting in an open-air theatre when an eagle flew over the stage. Eagles like to eat tortoises and when they catch one they drop it on a rock to smash its shell, so they can get to the nice gooey bits inside. This eagle, flying over the stage, thought Aeschylus's bald head was a rock. It dropped its tortoise on his head. The impact of the tortoise's shell killed him instantly.

I told Shakespeare this story and I swear his smile widened – as if he was laughing.

I just heard banging downstairs! It might really be evil men coming to take me away to the hospital! Or am I dreaming this too?

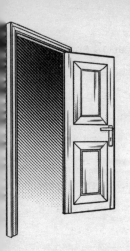
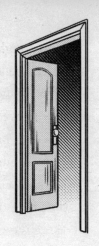

13

Gigantic Raindrops

Felix stepped back into the entrance hall of Murkhill Mansion and the gloom of the place hit her again.

'What should we do?' she asked Caspar.

'I don't know,' he replied. 'I guess we need to find Amelie's room – that's where all her rag toys will be. If all the strange stuff that's been happening is connected to them, then maybe they'll give us a clue about what is causing it all – and about what has happened to Drift.'

Felix walked over to the staircase. 'But when we found the door to Amelie's room it took us into the riddle. How are we going to get to her room when it could be behind any door in this mansion?'

'Don't know,' Caspar repeated. 'Wait. Did you hear that?'

'What?' asked Felix.

'It sounded like a bird's cry.'

'It's probably seagulls or something.'

Then Felix heard it. A sharp, piercing sound that

rang through the entrance hall, like no seagull she had ever heard.

She turned around. The statue of the eagle on the staircase wasn't a statue any more, it was alive. She stood, stunned, as the bird spread out its golden wings; they were huge – at least as wide as Felix was tall. With another cry and a furious flapping of wings the eagle took off. It soared near to the ceiling, its curved beak looking dangerously pointy as it stared down at her.

'Wow! A real eagle!'

'Duck, Felix!'

Caspar dived out of the way as something crashed down towards him.

Felix ran over – on the floor was an upside-down tortoise, the size of a football.

'That was close,' said Caspar.

Felix frowned at the tortoise, confused. Its legs started to wriggle in the air and Felix bent down and turned it the right way up. The tortoise slowly hobbled away.

'How exactly did that happen?' she asked.

'It's the eagles, they're— DUCK!' Caspar shouted.

Felix looked up just in time to see a second eagle hovering right above her, a tortoise in its talons. With an ear-splitting cry the eagle let the tortoise fall – rocketing straight towards Felix.

'What on earth?!' Felix threw herself backwards and the tortoise landed on the floor, centimetres away.

'It's from Amelie's imagination,' Caspar explained. 'She read about it in a book. A Greek actor died when an eagle dropped a tortoise on his head.'

'Why would it do that?'

'To try and smash the tortoise's shell. Amelie wrote in her diary that she told… Oh! I think I've just worked out what's—'

Another tortoise landed in front of Caspar. Felix froze as three more thudded to the floor around her. She looked down at them as they wriggled away, then she glanced up to the ceiling again. There were now at least twenty golden eagles flying around up there, their vast wingspans filling the whole space. Each had a tortoise in its talons, ready to drop.

'Run, Caspar, run!' she called, but her words were drowned out as all the eagles started to cry out at once. The sound rang through her ears. It felt like they were about to explode.

Tortoises began to fall all over the entrance hall, like gigantic raindrops. Felix charged towards Caspar and pushed him out through the front door.

They stood in the porch, listening to the sound of the eagles and the crashing tortoises inside the mansion.

Felix shook her head. 'This is crazy!'

'I think I've figured it out,' said Caspar. 'It's not just that those toys are connected to this weird stuff – I think one of the toys is making it all happen.'

'Shakespeare…' Felix realised.

Caspar nodded. 'Amelie told the Shakespeare rag toy all about the eagles and tortoises. And she told it about the snakes and ladders board and the riddle. It has been causing all this.'

'Shakespeare was a present from Mr Blaze, wasn't it?'

Caspar opened the diary to the first entry. 'And the note that went with the present said, "I hope this helps you to make your dreams come true." Mr Blaze must actually have meant that. He sent her the toy so that it could turn her dreams into reality. It did – and it still is!'

'But why are we being attacked?' asked Felix. 'Surely Amelie wouldn't want to hurt other children.'

'She was really scared about evil men coming to take her away, so maybe Shakespeare thinks we might be them and is using Amelie's imagination to protect her.'

'By creating the riddle and the snakes and ladders board…'

'And the cannon-ball tortoises,' Caspar added.

'Shakespeare must have thought Drift was trying to attack Amelie. We have to stop that toy and get Drift back,' said Felix.

Caspar looked at her and bit his lip. Then he stared at the diary. 'This all started happening when we pulled the diary out of the bookshelf. That was when the rooms started changing about. Shakespeare might have thought that we were stealing the diary. Maybe if we put it back, that will stop the rooms from being muddled.'

'Then we'll be able to find Amelie's room and the

Shakespeare toy. Good idea! So we need to get back to the library.'

She slowly opened the front door again. The floor of the entrance hall was now a maze of upside-down tortoises and, when she looked up, there were more eagles than Felix could count.

'I'll go in and try to distract the eagles. It'll give you time to get to the library door.' Felix stepped into the entrance hall and shouted, 'Oi, you lot! Over here!'

Sure enough, the eagles soaring overhead started to circle above her. Adrenalin pumped through Felix as she jumped over a pile of tortoises and weaved her way over to the right of the hallway – the opposite side to the library door.

'Go, Caspar, go!' She looked up and waved her arms at the eagles. 'I bet you can't get me!'

A barrage of tortoises were fired at her from the ceiling. Felix shuffled left and right to avoid the tortoises raining down around her. Across the hallway, Caspar was halfway to the library door.

The eagles soon replaced their weapons and Felix prepared herself. She leapt over to the staircase and pressed herself firmly against it. Seconds later, tortoises bounced off the banister above her.

She saw Caspar hesitating at the library door.

'You go in!' she called. 'Leave the door open and I'll follow you.'

Caspar disappeared through the doorway.

Felix started to weave her way around the tortoises by the staircase. A piercing cry, louder than any of the others, caught her attention. She looked up briefly — above her was a giant eagle, twice the size of the others. Felix felt her foot smash something hard and pain shot up her leg. Her other foot skidded along the floor and she fell backwards, landing in amongst the scattered tortoises.

Above her, the talons of the giant eagle opened and a tortoise flew down, heading straight for her head. All she could see was a ball of dark green getting bigger and bigger. In a second it would hit her. Thinking quickly, she grabbed a tortoise next to her and held it above her head.

She closed her eyes tightly and felt the thud as the falling tortoise hit the one in her hands and bounce away. She let out a sigh of relief and looked over at the fallen tortoise. It stared back with glazed eyes.

Felix stood up, but kept the tortoise held over her head. She made a run for the library, leaping over tortoises and kicking them out of the way. As she went, her heart beating madly, falling tortoises ricocheted off her tortoise. It was saving her from certain death.

Eventually she made it to the door. She placed the tortoise down, said a quick thank you to it and shot into the library. She closed the door to shut out the sound of the eagles' cries.

But the room behind the library door wasn't the

library. Of course it wasn't. It was another dark castle room with thick stone walls, empty save for a few features – set into the walls on both the left and the right were large fireplaces, and at the back of the room were the solid iron bars of a prison cell. There was a faint dripping sound from the ceiling and the room smelt dank. It looked like a dungeon.

There was no sign of Caspar, though.

'Caspar, where are you?'

'I'm in here, Felix.'

Out of the darkness of the prison cell, Caspar appeared. He grabbed hold of the bars and looked miserably out.

'I'm locked in here.'

14

July 7ᵗʰ 1965

Dear diary,

I have been trying to think of a way to keep myself busy - to keep my mind active so that I can forget my worries about Mum and Dad and evil men taking me away. Drawing is fine, but it doesn't take me long to make a picture and I have run out of things to draw.

Then I remembered: I have always wanted to write a play. But what could my play be about?

I spent a long time puzzling over it. Maybe I could turn one of the books I've read into a play, or one of my nightmares - they are pretty dramatic. In the end it was Shakespeare who gave me the answer. I grinned at him and he smiled back at me, and I wondered why Mr Blaze had sent him to me, and who exactly Mr Blaze was. As I looked at Shakespeare, ideas started to flood into my mind and a whole story began to form, about Mr Blaze giving Shakespeare special powers to really make people's dreams come true. I have never thought of an idea so quickly.

I set about writing this morning. The first scene takes place in my bedroom, on my birthday, when I received Shakespeare. Then the play travels back in time to show who Mr Blaze was and why he invented Shakespeare. Of course, it is all just a story – I have no way of knowing who Mr Blaze really is – but it has been fun imagining it.

I also had the idea that maybe one day my classmates can perform my play – all ten of them. In all the scenes involving me, I am in bed, so it might even be possible for me to act with my friends. Although if none of them came here on my birthday, I doubt any of them would want to act in my play.

I spent all day writing until it got dark outside and I felt exhausted. It had worked, though – I hadn't thought about any of my worries.

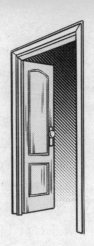

15

The Chimney

'How did you end up in there?' asked Felix.

'I was just looking inside it when the door swung shut,' said Caspar. 'I think this is the prison cell from Amelie's mind castle – she used it to lock all her nightmares away.'

'And you definitely can't get out?'

Caspar shook his head. His hands, clinging onto the bars, were shaking.

'I'm going to be trapped forever, like Drift, aren't I?'

'No,' Felix said firmly. 'I'll think of a way to get you out of there, then we'll find Drift.'

Felix found the cell's large iron door on the right. She tried pushing and pulling on it, but it wouldn't budge.

'There has to be a key to unlock it,' she said.

She moved over to the mantelpiece above one of the fireplaces and felt along it, but there was nothing. She went around the walls of the room to see if there was a key hanging up somewhere.

'Felix, through there.'

She looked at where Caspar was pointing. It was another doorway, next to the fireplace.

Felix frowned – the door was open. 'That wasn't there before, was it?'

'No, but look, there's a key.'

She walked over and peered through the doorway. The next room was more like a cupboard. It had the same medieval stone walls, but there was nothing inside it except a large key hanging on the far wall.

'Well spotted, Caspar.'

Felix went through the doorway. It was the biggest key she'd ever seen, twice the size of her hand and made of old, rusting iron – exactly the sort of key that would fit a medieval prison cell. She lifted it off the hook on the wall.

Her heart stopped as she heard the door slam shut. She wheeled around and heaved it open.

'Phew! I thought for a minute that I was going to get trapped too,' she said to Caspar.

But Caspar wasn't there any more. Neither was the prison cell. She was looking out at the living room they had been in earlier.

'Great!' she said sarcastically, walking into the room and kicking a vase over in frustration. 'I knew it was too easy, finding the key like that. It was just another trick, wasn't it?'

She had the key, but no way of knowing how to get back to the room with the prison cell.

'Why are you doing this? Why are you playing tricks on us?' she yelled at the mansion in general.

She breathed deeply in and out, trying to calm herself down. She had to find Caspar – before it was too late. Felix ran over to the door behind the sofa. Through it, she found herself in a long, thin room full of coats and dresses. They smelled old and musty. She brushed her way past them and found a door at the other end. It opened on to the room with all the paintings.

She walked over to one of Mr Blaze and glared up. 'Did you give Amelie that rag toy to help her, or to trick her? It trapped her parents somewhere, and her friend Elfie too – did you know that? Amelie was left there in her bed, all alone. And now that toy has trapped Drift somewhere and locked Caspar in the dungeon!'

Mr Blaze just stared out of the painting, his eyes black and sad.

Felix wanted to take the painting down and rip it into pieces, but she thought better of it. She didn't want to risk what might happen in this strange mansion if she did. She looked around the room and remembered that there was only the one door in and out – the one she had just come through.

She opened it again, but now the room behind it wasn't full of coats – it was the kitchen.

'Do the rooms change every time you shut the doors?' she wondered.

She closed the door and opened it again. Now it was

the toilet. Rather than having to run from room to room, she realised she could just open and close this door until she found the one with Caspar in.

The next time, there was a white-tiled bathroom. Then a medieval castle room; for a second she was excited, until she realised it wasn't the one with the prison cell – this one was full of shelves holding armour and weapons. Then a bedroom with a large double bed opposite a fireplace. Felix kept opening and closing the door, but she didn't find Caspar. She stopped when the same bedroom appeared again.

'Argh! This is hopeless. And anyway, if that Shakespeare rag toy is playing tricks on me, then it won't be this easy to find Caspar, let alone Drift.'

She stepped into the bedroom and looked around. Her eyes landed on the fireplace. She remembered there were a couple of fireplaces in the room Caspar was trapped in.

Felix had an idea. At home, there were two fireplaces – one in her mum's bedroom and one in the living room, and they were both connected to the same chimney. Maybe it was like that in this mansion too.

She bent down and peered inside the fireplace. It was heavily blackened by coal and soot, but if she squinted she saw the glow of light high above – the top of the chimney. Below was a hole leading down into pitch darkness. The chimney must be connected to other fireplaces on the floors below.

'I could climb down the chimney!'

Fireplaces weren't doors, so she hoped the rooms wouldn't be muddled up if she entered them through the fireplaces. Caspar's prison cell was in a dungeon, and that would probably be right at the bottom of the mansion.

With a renewed sense of determination, Felix squeezed herself backwards into the fireplace and dangled her feet into the chimney. She felt along the side of the chimney with her left foot, searching for something to grip onto, and found a groove to dig her foot into. She did the same with her right foot, then swung her whole body into the chimney. She was in! Felix started to edge her way downwards, using her feet to guide her down one side of the chimney, her back and hands firmly pressed against the other side to stop her falling. She couldn't see a thing. Felix loved climbing, but this was much harder than climbing a tree, or even down a cliff, and she gritted her teeth in concentration.

She was a few metres down when she heard a small rumble above her. A cold bubble of fear ran up Felix's throat – what if the chimney was about to collapse? The rumbling sound got closer and, seconds later, a pile of thick black soot landed on her face. She coughed and spluttered, trying to clear her throat, and wiped the soot away from her eyes with the back of a hand.

The rumbling stopped and Felix continued her descent. She soon came to a gap in the chimney where a dim beam of light shone in. Squinting out, she saw a study of some kind, with a desk and leather chair. Not Caspar. She kept shuffling down the chimney and the light faded. She found herself moving blindly and breathlessly. At least she was getting used to the climb now and found her footholds easily.

It seemed to take ages to arrive at the next fireplace. She looked out at the pantry they had been in earlier. That meant Felix was definitely going down the mansion in the right order – the pantry must be on the ground floor. Hopefully the dungeon was right below it.

A few minutes later, Felix's feet hit solid ground. She must be at the bottom of the chimney. She pushed away from the chimney wall and crawled into the fireplace, hoping she would see the dungeon.

'Hello?' she heard a small voice say. Caspar's voice.

She ducked out of the fireplace and grinned. There was Caspar, staring out at her from behind the bars of the prison cell, his mouth gaping open. Felix let out a sigh of relief.

'How did you get there?' Caspar asked.

Felix stood up straight and let her arms stretch out after the cramped chimney. 'Long story. But let's get you out of there.'

She took the key out of her pocket. It fitted easily into the cell lock and turned. The door was heavy, but with Felix pushing and Caspar pulling they got it open. Caspar stepped out.

'Thank you!' He went to hug Felix but quickly stopped. 'You're covered in soot.'

Felix looked down. Her T-shirt and jeans had changed colour – they were now completely black.

16

July 8th 1965

Dear diary,

I have finally found a way to get rid of my nightmares. Shakespeare has helped me. When I had all my bad dreams about Mum and Dad last night, I imagined him walking around my mind castle and scaring them away. He wasn't a small toy, though – I made him much bigger, even taller than Dad.

Although Shakespeare is always really happy and friendly with me, when he saw a nightmare happening in my mind castle, he looked really threatening with a menacing grin. It didn't scare me, though, because I knew he was trying to protect me. And it worked.

When the evil men came to take me to the hospital, Shakespeare trapped them in a giant game of snakes and ladders. When the dragon Mr Thrasher appeared, Shakespeare dealt with him easily, fighting the dragon's fire with lightning bolts shot from his eyes.

I managed to sleep through the whole night.

This morning I wrote the rest of my play about Shakespeare, imagining what it would be like if he really had the power to do what he did in my dreams. It's definitely the best thing I've ever written. The scene where Mr Blaze figures out how to give Shakespeare his powers is especially exciting. I don't know how to end the play, though. It has to end with Shakespeare granting me a wish, because in the play he really has the power to do that. But what wish do I want, more than any other?

This afternoon another present arrived - another rag toy. I sat it next to Hamlet and decided to call it Ophelia. Now five figures are sitting at the end of my bed, smiling at me.

They gave me an idea. I could draw a theatre for my play to be performed in. Not just on a single piece of paper, though - I pulled all the remaining pages out of my sketchpad and used them to make it really big. I drew a large stage, big red curtains and hundreds of seats. By the time I had finished, the theatre was spread out over my whole bed.

I was so eager to see my play performed that I started acting it out myself, imagining I was actually in the theatre I had drawn. I moved Shakespeare, Romeo, Juliet, Hamlet and Ophelia around as if they were the other actors. The only problem is there need to be five more actors to make the play work properly - I have written enough parts so that one day all ten of my classmates at school can act in it with me. So I just had to imagine five more rag-toys for now.

It was such a fun afternoon! I got so carried away that for a second I thought I really was performing the play and I even figured out what my most important wish is - the one that I ask Shakespeare to make come true at the end of the play. I wish my play could be performed for real, in an actual theatre with everyone on Thistlewick there to watch it. I love the thought of them all being entertained by Shakespeare's story. That's not my most important wish, though - it's my second biggest wish of all. My most important wish is far more important than that.

If only Shakespeare could make my most important wish come true in real life, not just in the play. I hope Mum and Dad come back into my room soon so I can tell them what it is.

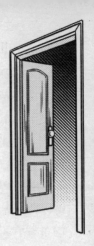

17

Mr Thrasher

'Do you still think that if we put the diary back in the bookshelf, it will stop the rooms from being mixed up?' asked Felix.

'I haven't got any better ideas,' Caspar replied. 'But how are we going to find the library?'

'There's a fireplace in the library, isn't there?'

Caspar nodded.

Felix looked from the fireplace she had just come through over to the one on the other side of the dungeon. 'The library fireplace wasn't connected to the chimney I've just climbed down, so it must be joined to the other one.'

'We've got to climb up that chimney?'

'The rooms are all in the correct order if you enter them through the fireplaces. The library should be on the floor above us, so it'll be easy enough.'

'If you say so.'

Felix went over and peered into the fireplace. It was

just as full of soot as the one she had climbed down. She looked up into the chimney and could only see darkness. There was no circle of light – maybe this chimney was blocked at the top by a bird's nest.

Out of nowhere came a ball of light, blinding Felix as it shot straight down the chimney. She blinked, trying to clear her eyes, and felt intense heat on her feet. She looked down and saw that a fire had started in the fireplace. Large orange flames were licking up her legs.

'Arrrgggh!' She jumped backwards.

'What caused that?' asked Caspar.

'Don't know!'

A deep rumbling noise sounded above them. It got louder and louder, making the floor shake under them.

'It sounds like the chimney's about to collapse!'

The rumbling got closer. Felix backed away from the fireplace, just as white-hot flames shot out of it, reaching far into the room like horizontal lightning. Felix threw herself to the floor just in time as the flames fired over her, straight towards Caspar. He jumped out of the way and the flames hit the wall, leaving a scorching brown mark in the place Caspar's head had been seconds before.

The flames cleared and Felix looked back at the fireplace. It took her a few seconds to realise what she was seeing.

'A dragon!'

Its red, snake-like head filled the whole fireplace.

Teeth the size of daggers protruded from its wide mouth and its eyes opened to reveal slits of pure blackness.

The dragon didn't seem to see Felix and Caspar at first. Still on the floor, Felix held her breath and tried not to make any sound that would attract its attention. But her heart was racing, making a loud thudding noise in her chest.

The dragon's large nostrils sniffed the air slowly, dangerously, as if searching for its prey. It started to climb out of the fireplace. Had it sensed them?

Felix's instinct was to run, but she didn't dare – a creature this size could reach out and gobble her in one bite. She edged her way slowly backwards to where Caspar stood frozen.

The dragon pushed its front legs out of the chimney, its sharp claws cracking the stone floor instantly. Its long tree-trunk of a neck stretched out over Felix as the dragon lurched towards Caspar. Felix looked up at the creature's scaly belly, and in between the scales a fiery orange glowed, emitting a burning heat.

The dragon's mouth was centimetres away from Caspar, whose eyes were wider than Felix had ever seen them. The dragon tilted its head sideways and sniffed. This wasn't like the snake attacking Drift earlier – it looked like the dragon was about to eat Caspar!

Thinking fast, Felix stretched her arms out and grabbed hold of Caspar's ankles. She pulled at them and he lost his balance and crashed to the floor. He was a dead weight, but Felix managed to heave him under the dragon's belly.

'Are you OK?' she whispered.

Caspar barely nodded. He held a hand up to protect his face from the heat of the dragon's belly.

The dragon flicked its tail angrily around, obviously wondering where its prey had disappeared to. As the tail hit the walls it sent stone shooting everywhere and dust flew into their faces.

'Where has this dragon come from?' mouthed Felix.

'It must be Mr Thrasher.'

'Mr Thrasher?'

'From Amelie's nightmares. She imagined her head teacher turning into a dragon and tried to lock him away in her mind castle.'

The dragon opened up its wings now, blasting air about as they filled the entire room, like the out-of-control wings of an aeroplane. Felix felt her skin burning as the dragon swung its whole body around, sending sparks of fire flying everywhere. She rolled sideways, just avoiding a claw the size of her arm as the dragon stepped over her.

The rumbling sound started again, but now it was directly above Felix and Caspar – it came from the dragon's belly. The cracks in the belly glowed orange, then red, then white. Sweat poured down Felix's face in the unbearable heat.

The glow of fire travelled up the dragon, along its

neck and shot out of its mouth with an ear-splitting shriek. Flames soared through the room, circling around the dragon as it flicked its tail and flapped its wings. The temperature got even hotter.

'We're going to be eaten, aren't we?' cried Caspar, no longer whispering.

'What did Amelie say Mr Thrasher got angry with her about?' asked Felix, an idea forming in her mind.

'He … he thought she was cheating in a test.'

'Right, give me the diary.'

Felix took it from Caspar's shaking hand. She turned to the back, found an empty page and ripped it out of the diary.

'What are you doing?' asked Caspar.

'You'll see.'

Felix rolled out from under the dragon and stood up next to its tail. Careful not to touch the green spikes, she yanked on the tail and the dragon's neck whipped round. She was suddenly face to face with the beast. It bared its razor-sharp teeth at her – one bite would cut her in half – but she tried to keep her cool.

'Oi, Mr Thrasher, look! I've been cheating on my test.'

She held up the piece of paper. The dragon sniffed at it, smoke billowing out of its nostrils. It blinked. Felix knew if this didn't work, she was toast.

She flinched as the dragon let out a shattering wail, its mouth open wide, revealing rows of vicious teeth and a forked tongue. She had definitely made it angry. It raised its head up, but Felix was already running along the side of the room.

She reached the prison cell Caspar had been in.

'Mr Thrasher, over here!'

The dragon turned, the swish of its tail on the wall sending several large bits of stone clanging into the bars of the cell. It stomped over to Felix.

She screwed the piece of paper up and chucked it inside the cell. Then she threw herself out of the way as the dragon charged after the paper like a dog chasing a stick. It squeezed its way into the prison cell, wings clattering against the bars.

'Quick, Caspar, help me close the door!'

Caspar ran over and together they swung the thick iron door of the prison cell shut. Felix put the key in the lock and took a deep breath in relief as she turned it.

The dragon spat a ball of fire in their direction but the fire hit the iron door and petered out harmlessly.

'Let's get out of here before anything else tries to stop us!' Felix ran over to the fireplace the dragon had come through. 'Come on, Caspar, you go up first.'

She helped him into the fireplace and pushed him up. His legs were shaking uncontrollably.

'Just take it easy, Caspar.'

'Ok, I've got a grip. It looks like the dragon knocked out some of these bricks, so there's loads of gaps to hold onto.'

'Great. Pull yourself up, then push your back against one side of the chimney and use your feet to climb up the other.'

Felix watched him disappear up into the chimney. She looked back to the prison cell. The dragon stared grumpily out at her. It flicked its tail against the bars, making them clang.

'Nice meeting you, Mr Thrasher!' She grinned at the dragon, then bent down into the fireplace.

Caspar was right. There were plenty of gaps in the brickwork and it made climbing up the chimney really easy. She quickly caught up with him.

Soon, Caspar came to a halt. 'Here's an opening… You're right, Felix, it's the library.'

In no time at all they squeezed out of the fireplace.

Felix smiled at Caspar, now covered in soot too. 'I've never seen you looking so dirty!'

'Come on, let's put the diary back,' he said.

Caspar went over to the bookcase with all the white books in it. Felix watched as he found the gap for the diary. He pushed it into place.

But as he did so, Caspar yelled out. He looked back to Felix, his mouth open in shock. Then, he vanished into thin air.

'Caspar!'

Felix ran forwards. She found the diary back in its place on the shelf, but Caspar was nowhere to be seen.

What had happened to him? Where had he gone?

As Caspar had disappeared putting the diary back, Felix decided to pull it out again. Nothing happened.

She stared from the diary in her hand to the gap in the bookshelf. What if returning the diary to the shelf had taken Caspar to wherever Drift had gone when he had disappeared? There was one way to find out.

Gritting her teeth, Felix plunged the diary back into the bookcase.

'Aaahhh!'

A pain ran up her arm, like a giant electric shock. She tried to let go of the book, but her hand was stuck to it. The electric shock spread through her body and she writhed around, trying to stop the terrible feeling. But it was no good.

The room around her started to fade and Felix was thrown forwards into complete darkness.

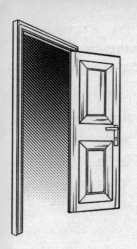
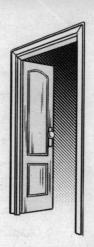

18

The Red Room

Felix's feet landed on solid ground. She tumbled forwards in the pitch black and hit her knee on something very hard.

'Owww!'

The sound echoed eerily around her.

From somewhere nearby a voice said, 'Felix?'

'Caspar!'

She put her arms out in front of her and moved slowly towards where his voice had come from. Her left hand touched something warm – a shoulder.

'Did you pull out the diary again?' he asked.

'Yes. Then I put it back in – and got shot through to here. Where are we?'

'No idea! But I don't think putting the diary back worked. This mansion is still playing tricks on us.'

'Where are we?' asked Felix.

A moment later, her question was answered. Lights started to flicker on around them, stretching further and further until a vast space was soon revealed.

Felix blinked and, as her eyes focused, she saw a sea of rich red and golden colours flowing out in front of her, splashing around every corner of the giant room, lapping up the walls and filling her mind. She felt breathless at the sight. It was a while before she could take in any of the details.

Rows and rows of plush red seats stretched out along an equally red carpet, all pointing in the same direction to a raised stage far above them. A huge red curtain, the biggest Felix had ever seen, hung between two golden pillars at the back of the stage.

At the top of the stage was a sculpture of a golden smiley face, at least as tall as Felix's whole body and shining brilliantly – just like the one on the front door of Murkhill Mansion.

'This is a theatre, isn't it?' She looked over to Caspar and he was wide-eyed in wonder.

'It's Amelie's theatre,' he replied. 'The one she talked about drawing in her last diary entry. Shakespeare must have created it for her, so that her play can be performed. It was her second biggest wish.'

They walked towards the stage, then climbed up the steps. They stood in front of the curtain, looking out over the ocean of seats below.

'There must be room for hundreds of people in here,' said Felix.

'Room for the whole of Thistlewick,' said Caspar.

'Amelie wanted everyone on Thistlewick to come and see her play. So … what do we do now?'

'Let's have a look behind there.'

Felix turned around to the curtain and felt along it, searching for the gap in the middle. She found it and poked her head through.

Behind it she saw a bedroom. It must be the mansion playing tricks on her again, taking her to a different room. She wasn't falling for that.

But as she looked closely she quickly realised that this wasn't just any bedroom. Machines with wires coming out of them stood to one side of the bed and the walls were covered in drawings.

'Caspar, look – it's Amelie's room!'

Caspar poked his head through the curtain beside her. 'Is Shakespeare in here?'

They stepped through. Felix went straight over to the bed, but there was no sign of Shakespeare, or of any of the other rag toys. Spread out over the bed, though, were Amelie's drawings of her imagined theatre – identical to the theatre Felix and Caspar had just been in.

What's more, lying on the pillow was a red book. Amelie's diary, with the nine scratches on its cover! How had it got from the library into Amelie's room?

Felix picked it up and took it over to show Caspar. He was standing close to a wall, tapping on it.

'What are you doing?'

'This isn't a real wall. It's just a thin piece of wood.'

Felix frowned. She walked over to the window on the other side of the room. But it wasn't a window – just a really good painting of one, looking out onto a painted view of the sea.

'This isn't a room, it's a set,' Caspar realised. 'I think we're still on the stage in the theatre.'

'But it looks just like a real bedroom. Like Amelie's bedroom.' Felix peered back out of the stage curtain – all the red seats were there. 'Yes, we're still in the theatre.'

'The Shakespeare toy must have copied everything from Amelie's room exactly, just like he copied her drawing of the theatre and all her other ideas. Amelie's bedroom must be the set for her play.'

'But if Shakespeare copied everything, where is *he*? There isn't a copy of him or the other rag toys on Amelie's bed.'

'Felix…' Caspar was staring directly behind her.

She turned around slowly.

Out of a shadow in the corner of the set stepped a figure, wrapped in a long black cloak that stretched to the floor. One of the rag toys. But it wasn't toy-sized, it was almost twice the height of Felix. She saw its name badge – this was Shakespeare. Its golden, mask-shaped face smiled at her warmly, its deep black eyes drawing her in.

She felt very happy.

'Hello, Shakespeare,' she said, starting to move towards him.

He couldn't have made all the creepy things in the mansion happen, she thought. *He's only an innocent, friendly toy.*

Felix shook her head to clear her mind. Those weren't her thoughts. Was Shakespeare hypnotising her? Is that what he had done to Amelie, to make her feel happy?

'Where is Drift?' Felix asked Shakespeare. 'What have you done to him?'

Shakespeare tilted his mask-head sideways. With his smile fixed on Felix, she knew he was trying to make her think happy thoughts. But she clenched her fists and resisted him.

'Answer me!' she shouted.

Suddenly, Shakespeare changed. His mask flashed from golden to blood red. His eyes glowed an even brighter red and his smile twisted into a terrifying, evil grin. He looked nothing like a toy now – he was a monster!

The monster-Shakespeare glided forwards towards Felix as she stared at him in horror.

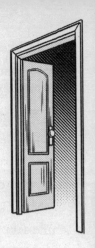

19

The Dance

Felix grabbed Caspar's hand and pulled him backwards as the monster-Shakespeare approached.

Out of a shadow in the opposite corner of the set a second figure appeared. A monster almost identical to Shakespeare, red-faced, with the same scary grin stretched across it – except this one was smaller. Felix looked at its name badge – Amelie had called it Titania.

The two monsters crept slowly towards Felix and Caspar. Felix felt Caspar's hand trembling under her grip, and could no longer suppress her own fear. The monsters were now barely a metre away.

Shakespeare raised an arm and held his hand out towards Felix. But no, she saw it wasn't a hand, it was a claw, sharp and pointed, like a bird's. She flinched, but then Shakespeare moved it to point at the monster next to him.

'Are you trying to tell me something?' asked Felix.

'I think … he's answering your question,' said Caspar.

She frowned, not understanding, but saw Caspar's face grow tense in horror. Then she turned towards the other monster, Titania, and realised. It wasn't just smaller than Shakespeare, it was almost half his size, the same height as Felix – the same height as…

'Drift… No! It can't be! You've turned him into one of you?!' Felix felt like she had been punched in the stomach.

'Amelie wished she had more friends like Shakespeare,' Caspar said gravely. 'That's what he's done.'

Stunned, Felix followed Shakespeare's arm as it moved towards the giant red curtains. They flung dramatically open to reveal several more monsters sitting in the front row of seats. Felix stared at the identical cruel grins on their blood-red faces, at their eyes like two holes leading to hell. She realised who they must be…

'Everyone who's got trapped here – Dr Ralph, Elfie, Amelie's parents – you turned them all into monsters like you!'

She looked from the monsters in the audience to the two onstage, which swept towards her, their black cloaks blowing around as if caught up in some invisible wind. Felix and Caspar had no choice but to edge backwards towards the audience. Try as she might, Felix couldn't take her eyes off the monsters' faces, which tilted from side to side as they moved, like demonic versions of curious dogs. She moved her left foot back and it landed on thin air – she had reached the edge of the stage. Felix swayed, trying to control her balance as the monster moved ever closer. But she couldn't help toppling and fell from the stage, Caspar crashing down with her. They landed heavily on the floor below.

Before Felix could try to get up, the monsters that had been sitting in the seats stood up, staring at them, and the two from the stage climbed down and pointed at Felix and Caspar.

'What … do we do?' Caspar asked through sharp breaths, sprawled on the floor.

'Don't know.' Felix got to her feet, not ready to give up. 'We have to find a way to get Drift back!'

Five monsters now surrounded them. They were completely trapped. Felix felt herself being sucked in by their eyes again and looked down, trying to control her horror so that she could think. She saw the diary in her hand.

It had worked with the dragon, but would it work with these monsters?

'Oi, you lot, fetch!'

She threw the diary hard to her left. The monsters didn't move, but they turned to look. Felix grabbed Caspar's arm and pulled him in between two of the monsters. They reached the aisle at the centre of the seats.

'We have to get out of here!'

'Let's try at the back, where we came in,' Caspar suggested.

They ran up the aisle to the back of the theatre. It was just a solid wall – no doors, nothing.

A whooshing sound behind them made Felix and Caspar swing around. The monsters weren't at the front any more. All five were now high above the seats, using their cloaks as wings, like giant bats, as they soared towards Felix and Caspar!

They froze as the monsters landed in front of them. Felix looked at the five monsters and found Shakespeare standing in the middle. She spoke to him as calmly as possible.

'Please. We're just children, like Amelie, and she wouldn't want you to harm us. Give Drift back to us and we'll leave Murkhill Mansion and never come back. I promise.'

Shakespeare stared back at her. His mask-face seemed to soften, the redness dimmed.

'Please,' she said.

As one, all five monsters raised their arms, pointing sharp claws at Felix. Their evil grins widened and a menacing hiss filled the air.

Caspar backed away against the wall. 'If Shakespeare turned Amelie's parents into these things, then we don't stand a chance.'

'Come on!' Felix tugged at him and they started to run – just in time, because one of the monsters was reaching out an arm to grab them.

They made it to the left-hand corner of the theatre,

but whooshing filled the air as the monsters followed. Felix let out a gasp as more monsters appeared out of a shadow on their other side – they were trapped in the corner. Felix and Caspar squeezed tightly together, Felix now trembling as much as her friend.

Felix counted nine monsters surrounding them, and remembered the nine scratches in the diary. These were – or had been – all the people who had got trapped in the mansion!

'Drift?' she asked. 'Where is Drift?'

The monsters all turned to face each other, then the one with Titania written on its name badge stepped forwards.

'Drift? Is that really you?'

The monster's mask-face tilted from side to side as it moved to within touching distance.

Without thinking about it, Felix lunged forwards and grabbed hold of either side of the mask-face. She yanked it, trying to rip it off her friend. The eyes in the mask glowed white and sparked, but she still held on. Then two bolts of electricity shot out of them and fired into Felix.

'Aaahhh!' Felix flew backwards, hit the wall and slid down into a heap on the floor.

'Felix!' she heard Caspar cry.

She blinked but her mind was spinning. She shook her head, trying to clear it. As her vision came back into focus, she saw the monsters surrounding Caspar.

'No! Get away from him!' she called.

One of the monsters turned around. Felix felt a rising sickness as the monster swept towards her with its menacing grin.

She could do nothing as it grabbed at her waist and lifted her up over its shoulder. Its cloak billowed and it flew high into the air. Felix closed her eyes as a rush of coldness flew past her.

A second later, her eyes jolted open as they landed and she was thrust into a seat at the front of the theatre. The monster forced her left hand onto the arm of the seat and, with a gnarled claw, it drew a circle of electric blue light in the air around her hand. Felix tried to struggle – to move her hand – but as soon at it got near the electricity a searing pain ran up her arm. The monster did the same to her other hand. She was stuck there, restrained by electric handcuffs.

The other monsters were now up on the stage with Caspar. Felix desperately tried to see him among them. She made him out at the centre, collapsed on the ground and cowering.

The lights around the theatre dimmed, replaced by two powerful spotlights, which flooded the stage in pure whiteness.

All nine monsters started doing a strange sort of dance in a circle around Caspar. Felix couldn't see their feet under the cloaks, but she heard them stamping on the stage.

Stamp! Stamp! Stamp!

It was so loud it felt like there were far more than nine monsters. Their evil red faces twitched in rhythm to the sound.

Stamp! Stamp! Stamp!

Felix didn't know what to do. Through the stamping she could just hear Caspar's cries. Between the cloaks she could just see him crumpled on the floor, his eyes tight shut.

She tried wriggling her right hand out of the electric handcuff.

'Aaarrrgggh!' The shock was unbearable, like touching an electric eel.

Her mind was determined to rip her arm away and rescue Caspar, but her body was too afraid of the electricity. Her arms tensed up and refused to move.

Stamp! Stamp! STAMP!

As the monsters circled Caspar, closer and closer. Felix guessed he was seconds away from being turned into one of them.

She tried once more to free herself from the electric handcuffs, but her hands just gripped onto the arms of the seat and shook.

'Come on!' she yelled. She thought about how it was all her fault they were in this situation. She had been the one who'd decided to come to Murkhill Mansion. Caspar hadn't even wanted to enter the place. Drift had already changed, but she would never forgive herself if she didn't try to stop the monsters from changing Caspar.

With one huge roar of determination she forced her arms up. They passed through the handcuffs and her whole body shook. It felt like all the world's lightning was running through her. She fell forwards and collapsed in agony on the floor, her wrists burning.

She was brought to her senses by a voice calling out, 'Help! Help!'

'Caspar!'

Felix stood up and ran towards the steps leading to the stage. The monsters were so closely packed around Caspar now that she could no longer see him. She climbed the first step, her heart rate increasing. Step by step it got faster and faster. Then she realised her heart was beating in exact time with the monsters' stamping.

Stamp-stamp! Stamp-stamp!

She reached the final step and the stamping immediately stopped. Her own heartbeat stopped too.

'AAAAAAAAAAAHHHHHHHHHH!'

Caspar's ear-splitting scream rang through the theatre.

'Caspar!' Felix's heartbeat started again.

She charged at the ring of monsters. But before she reached them, they began to spread outwards. Through the centre of them a figure moved forwards. It was shrouded in a black cloak, its face glowed red and its grin was just as horrible as the others'. This one, with the name badge Oberon, was the smallest out of all of them.

Felix gasped. 'Caspar?'

She counted, and sank to her knees – there were now ten monsters.

'No no no! Caspar! What have they done to you?'

The expression on the monster that had been Caspar didn't change. Its face twitched, showing the faintest glimmer of recognition. But the monster-Caspar kept on moving towards Felix, its evil eyes fixed on her.

The other monsters started to hiss, and she realised they were hissing her name.

'*Fe-lix!*'

The monster-Caspar was getting closer.

'*Fe-lix!*'

Closer.

'*Fe-lix! Fe-lix!*'

The chanting got faster and faster. The monster drew closer still. There was nothing Felix could do. Drift had changed and now Caspar had too.

'*Fe-lix! Fe-lix!*'

The monster was so close now that Felix could see the tears filling her eyes reflected in its red face.

'Caspar, please!'

'*Fe-lix! Fe-lix!*'

The face got bigger. Suddenly it was twice the size of her, its piercing eyes glaring down.

'FE-LIX!'

The giant red face opened its mouth wide. It shot towards her, she feared about to eat her up. All the sounds became one long, unbearable scream. And then...

Darkness.

Silence.

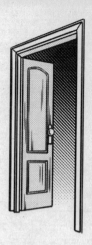

20

Amelie's Second Biggest Wish

Felix opened her eyes a crack.

She was surrounded by flowers. But no, they weren't flowers, just pictures of them. Pictures painted onto bed sheets. She opened her eyes fully and realised she was tucked under the duvet of Amelie's bed – or at least the copy of her bed on the stage in the theatre. Over to her right was the huge red curtain, now closed again.

Felix squinted at her watch. It was 9 a.m. on 23rd July. She'd been asleep all night!

She sat bolt upright as everything that had happened came flooding back. Had she dreamt about Caspar being turned into a theatre-mask monster? She looked around the bed and found the copy of the diary on the bedside cabinet. She grabbed hold of it and counted the scratches.

Ten. So it was real – Caspar had been changed. Felix groaned.

But why hadn't she been changed? The last thing she

remembered was one of the monsters coming straight for her. Why had Shakespeare turned Drift and Caspar into monsters but not her?

A shadow formed over the duvet and Felix slowly looked up, fearful of what would greet her. But the monster standing at the end of the bed had its golden, happy face once again. Shakespeare.

For an instant, Felix forgot all about Drift and Caspar and felt content in this nice warm bed.

'No! I won't let you hypnotise me, or whatever it is you did to Amelie.' Felix kicked the duvet and climbed out of the bed. 'I'm going to get out of here. I'm going to find a way to make you stop – and get Drift and Caspar and all the others back!'

As she said it, Felix realised she had no idea how she could do this, or if it was even possible.

Shakespeare hissed, his face changing from gold to red. It twitched and grinned a wide, evil grin at her.

She ran for the curtain. But another of the monsters appeared through it, right in front of her, twitching like Shakespeare. It raised its arms, revealing sharp claws.

Felix knew she wouldn't be able to escape like that.

'So,' she said, looking back to Shakespeare by the bed, 'why didn't you turn me into one of you?'

Shakespeare stopped twitching and his face changed back to the golden smile. He took the diary Felix had left on the bed and opened it to a page towards the end. He looked from the book to Felix and back again.

'You want me to read it?' She moved warily over to the bed.

Shakespeare held out a sharp claw and Felix flinched. But he wasn't aiming it at her, he was using it to point to words in Amelie's diary: 'I started acting out my play, imagining I was actually in the theatre.'

Felix looked at Shakespeare. 'You want to make Amelie's imagination come true, I get it. That's why you made this theatre.'

Shakespeare pointed to a different part of Amelie's writing: 'I moved Shakespeare, Romeo, Juliet, Hamlet and Ophelia around as if they were the other actors. The only problem is there need to be five more actors to make the play work properly.'

'So Amelie wanted ten actors in her play. When she was pretending to act it out, she had five rag toys and imagined there were five more. That's why you've been turning people into rag toys – so that there are enough of you to act in Amelie's play.'

Shakespeare looked at Felix and his head tilted up and down.

'And now there *are* enough of you.'

Shakespeare's claw moved to a bit of writing on the final page of Amelie's diary: 'I wish that it could be performed for real, in an actual theatre with everyone on Thistlewick there to watch.'

Shakespeare tapped on the word 'everyone'.

'So, you want to make Amelie's wish come true and

perform her play, and you want everyone on Thistlewick to come and watch it?'

He tapped on 'everyone' again, then pointed his claw directly at Felix.

'And you want me to get everyone to come to the theatre?' She thought for a minute. 'But how am I supposed to do that? The council are about to demolish Murkhill Mansion. Do you really think they would listen to me if I asked them to come inside and watch a play?'

Shakespeare glared at her and his eyes flashed dangerously red.

'OK, OK, I'll do it. But only if you agree to do something for me. When the performance is over, you've got to turn Caspar and Drift and all the other monsters back to normal. That is my wish, and I think it would be Amelie's wish too.'

Shakespeare just smiled at her, in his fixed, happy way. Two other monsters appeared from the shadows at the side of the stage and she let them take hold of her arms. She was lifted up, her legs dangling, and they carried her through the curtains, off the stage and into the aisle between the seats. They both pointed towards the back of the theatre, where Felix saw a door that hadn't been there before. Shakespeare was letting her escape.

She walked quickly up the aisle, without a clue about how she could get everyone on Thistlewick to come and watch the monsters perform. Her mind spun as she thought about her friends. How on earth was she going to get them back to normal? She turned the handle on the door. It opened. She was once again thrown into darkness.

A second later she fell forwards and landed on the carpet in the library. She ran to the library door and it opened out onto the entrance hall.

Shakespeare was definitely letting her out of Murkhill Mansion. She could run away now and never come back. But no way was she going to leave Caspar and Drift trapped in there.

She heard a loud rumbling noise from outside then that echoed around the entrance hall.

'Oh no!'

The bulldozers and wrecking balls must have arrived – Felix didn't have much time. She had to find a way to stop Shakespeare before Murkhill Mansion was knocked down!

She heaved open the front door.

The bright morning sunlight spread over the entrance hall, momentarily blinding her.

As it cleared she saw two men and a woman dressed in yellow jackets. One of the men turned towards the front door. 'What on earth…?'

'What is it?' asked Mayor Merryweather, coming to join the workers. His eyes fell on Felix standing in the doorway.

The mayor's moustache twitched as he took in the

sight of her. Then his eyes widened in surprise. 'Felix, what are you doing in there?'

She was thinking of an answer when she looked past Mayor Merryweather.

Just the other side of the garden gate a number of other workers in bright yellow jackets stood around a few big machines. Stretching out into the distance behind them, though, were hundreds of Thistlewickians.

Felix's mouth fell open. Mayor Merryweather really had made a big event out of the demolition. It looked like the whole of Thistlewick was here to see it happen.

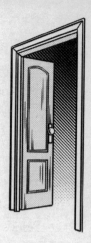

21

The Bulldozer

Felix gulped as she saw her mum pushing through the crowd to join Mayor Merryweather and the three workers.

'Did I hear you saying my daughter's name?'

Mayor Merryweather pointed at Felix. Mum turned and her eyes grew huge.

'Felix!' Concern and confusion mixed with the anger on her face.

'Hi, Mum,' Felix said in a small voice.

'I've been worried sick. Where have you been all night?'

'I ... I was in Murkhill Mansion.'

Felix prepared herself for the telling-off she was about to get.

'Felix Dashwood, I cannot—'

But Mum was interrupted by one of the workers.

'Mayor Merryweather, this is against all regulations,' he said. 'How could you allow a child to go inside

Murkhill Mansion? And she was in there overnight?! The place could have collapsed on top of her.'

The mayor glared at Felix. 'I assure you, I did not know anything about this.'

'We could have knocked this place down today without even knowing she was in there. We could have killed her. Did you not make the checks of the mansion, like we asked you to?'

'Well, you see, we don't really go inside Murkhill Mansion. It has a ... reputation.'

'So you had no way of knowing if anyone was in there? I think this is a matter for the police.' The workman reached into his pocket and took out a mobile phone.

'Steady on,' said Felix's mum. 'Why don't you let my daughter explain what she was doing in there?'

'She can tell her story to the police.' The workman started dialling a number.

'For goodness' sake!' Mum turned to the man and started yelling, seemingly directing all the anger she felt towards Felix at him instead.

Felix looked out at all the other people surrounding Murkhill Mansion. They were all staring in one direction, to the right side of the building. Felix turned around and gasped as she took in the great beast of a machine being driven up to it. A bulldozer, at least half the size of the mansion and glowing bright yellow. Behind it was another beast, with a huge black wrecking ball swinging in front of it. Realisation struck. These were the machines that would destroy Murkhill Mansion – with Caspar and Drift still stuck inside!

Felix's eyes darted around as she desperately tried to think of something she could do to stop this from happening. Mum, Mayor Merryweather and the workers were now in a heated argument. Maybe, if she could get the crowd's attention, she could persuade them to come into Murkhill Mansion and watch Amelie's play, like Shakespeare wanted.

She ran away from the mansion, jumped over the garden fence and pushed through the crowd, heading right towards the machines. She could hear the cries of people around her, but they were muffled, as if Felix was surrounded by an invisible bubble.

Felix ran towards the big yellow bulldozer, and was faintly aware of men in yellow jackets reaching out to stop her. Their hands barely touched her as she made a flying leap for the front of the bulldozer. She hit it heavily and her bubble burst.

Now she heard the crowd behind her, and the gruff voices of the workers close by.

'What's she doing?'

'Get down, girl!'

But nothing was going to stop her. Felix scrambled up onto the front of the bulldozer and, gripping the open side door, pulled herself on top of the machine, right at the front of it. She turned around to face the crowd and felt the sun hit her. There was no time to feel nervous. She had everyone's attention.

'Fifty years ago a girl called Amelie Summercroft lived in this mansion,' she began loudly.

'Who is that up there?'

'What's she saying?'

Felix continued, even louder, 'Amelie always dreamed of having her play performed to everyone on Thistlewick.'

She looked down and saw Mum and Mayor Merryweather break away from their argument with the workers.

'Felix, get down from there this instant!' Mum called.

'A theatre has been built inside Murkhill Mansion especially to perform Amelie's play.'

Mayor Merryweather frowned. 'There is no theatre in there. How can there be?'

Felix looked around at the hundreds of islanders stretched out in front of the bulldozer, all staring directly at her.

'We would like you all to help make Amelie's wish come true. Please come with me into Murkhill Mansion and watch a performance of Amelie's play.'

She started to climb down from the bulldozer. The workers stood around her, speechless, while the crowd exploded into a thousand voices. Eventually one of the workers stepped forwards and gave Felix a hand down. Her heart in her mouth, she looked around at the islanders, unsure whether what she had said had worked.

Were they talking excitedly, or angrily? She walked back to the entrance of Murkhill Mansion.

'*We?*' asked Mayor Merryweather through gritted teeth. 'You said "we".'

'Exactly how many people are inside Murkhill Mansion, Felix?' asked Mum.

The islanders pressed forwards towards the mansion, but the workers stood in front of the garden gate, stopping them from getting too close.

'There are ten others,' Felix replied.

'Ten!' The workman with the mobile raised his arms in disbelief.

Two people managed to break through the line of workers. They ran into the garden. It was Caspar's mum and Drift's dad.

Felix felt a pang of guilt as she saw the panicked expressions on their faces.

'Is Caspar in there?' asked his mum.

'And Drift?' asked his dad.

Felix nodded, unsure what to say. She couldn't exactly tell them what had happened to their children.

'I will give you five minutes to get those kids out of there,' the workman with the mobile said to Mayor Merryweather, 'or else I'm calling the police.'

Felix realised she needed to do something dramatic to get everyone past the workers and inside.

She stepped back through the main entrance of Murkhill Mansion.

'Felix! What are you doing?' yelled Mum.

'Come back here!' called the mayor.

She glanced back at them. 'Catch me if you can!'

Felix turned and ran through the entrance hall and into the library. She positioned herself just behind the door and waited. Through the doorway charged Mum, Mayor Merryweather and Drift and Caspar's parents.

'Where has she gone?' asked the mayor.

Felix stepped forwards and grabbed hold of his arm, taking him by surprise. As he yelled at her to let go, she dragged him over to the bookcase, pulled out Amelie's diary and then put it back in. She prepared herself to be thrown forwards into darkness with the mayor. But nothing happened.

She frowned and pulled the diary out and put it back again. Nothing.

'Felix, stop this now!' said Mayor Merryweather.

She dropped his arm and stepped back. Why wasn't Shakespeare letting her into the theatre?

'You are in so much trouble right now, Fe—'

But Mum stopped as the bookcase suddenly slid sideways.

Behind it, Felix saw a large, grand door, surrounded by a border of shining, flashing lights and above it a sign: 'Amelie's Theatre'.

Shakespeare had created a proper entrance.

Felix looked at Mayor Merryweather. 'I told you. Come on, let me show you.'

The door opened without her turning the handle. She walked in and the adults followed her cautiously.

The theatre was fully lit. Spread out in front of them were the many royal-red seats and the stage with the huge curtain stretched across it.

'My goodness!' said Caspar's mum breathlessly.

'Felix, you … you were telling the truth,' said Mum in surprise.

Felix turned back to face the adults. 'Please, bring everyone else in. It was Amelie's second biggest wish for the whole of Thistlewick to watch her play being performed.'

The mayor took in the theatre, but then shook his head sadly. 'I am sorry, Felix. The machines are ready to demolish Murkhill Mansion. It has stood here uninhabited for too long. And you heard what the workers said – if we don't get you and your friends out of here, they will call the police. Theatre or no theatre, it is time for Murkhill Mansion to be knocked down.'

'Please!' Felix pleaded. 'You don't realise how important it is that you watch this play.'

Mayor Merryweather's moustache perked up and turned into a beaming smile. 'Actually, I think that is an excellent idea.'

'You … you do?' asked Felix, confused by his sudden change of mind.

'Yes, don't you agree, Mrs Dashwood?'

'I certainly do,' said Mum.

'Let's go and fetch everyone else. They've got to see this place!' said Oakley Castle.

As one, they all turned around and walked back out into the library.

Felix stood there, baffled – until she sensed something behind her. All ten monsters were standing there in a row, with golden, happy faces.

'You hypnotised them, didn't you? That's why they changed their minds so quickly. They want to watch the play because you made them want to.'

The ten monsters smiled an identical, happy smile at her.

Footsteps echoed around the entrance hall of Murkhill Mansion as people filed in, and Felix felt a bolt of doubt shoot through her.

Just about everyone on Thistlewick would be coming into the theatre. What if this was actually part of a bigger trick that Shakespeare was pulling? What if he wanted everyone to come in not because it was Amelie's wish, but so that he could change all of them into theatre-mask monsters too?

The first few people entered the theatre. It was too late to worry now.

'Wow! This is amazing!' said Mr Finch.

'Spectacular,' trilled Mrs Didsbury.

Felix looked straight at one of the monsters. 'Remember our deal. I've got everyone to come in and watch Amelie's play. Once you've performed it, you will let all these people go free and turn Caspar, Drift and the others back to normal. Yes?'

The monster made no indication that it had agreed to this. It stepped forwards, put its arm around Felix's waist and lifted her up. She knew it was hopeless to struggle against it. The monster shot up into the air and flew quickly over the seats, making Felix dizzy. They landed on the stage and disappeared behind the big red curtain.

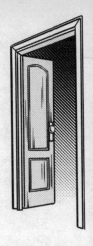

22

The Performance

The monster dropped Felix down on the stage. He pointed towards the bed on the set of Amelie's room. Felix nodded, not daring to disobey, and got in. Another monster handed her a notebook. She opened it – it was Amelie's play.

'So that's why you didn't turn me into one of you! You want me to play Amelie.'

The monster tilted its head up and down, then walked into the shadows and disappeared. All the other monsters followed it.

Felix was left lying in the bed, unsure of what to do. She had never really acted before. She heard excited talking from the other side of the curtain getting louder and louder as the seats filled up.

A few minutes later, silence fell and the curtains slowly opened. In the dim light, Felix could just see the audience. It really looked like the whole of Thistlewick was there – every seat was taken. All except one, left empty in the front row, in between Mayor Merryweather and Felix's mum.

A powerful spotlight hit Felix and she realised she had to begin.

She gulped and looked down at the first page of the notebook to see what was meant to happen. She read the title, 'Scene 1: Amelie's Room', and realised that the play opened with her talking to the audience.

She cleared her throat and began, 'My name is Amelie Summercroft and I have just turned ten years old. I live in Murkhill Mansion with my mum and dad. As you can see, I am confined to my bed, but my parents made sure I had a brilliant tenth birthday. My favourite present was a rag toy with a golden, smiley face. I named him Shakespeare.'

The monster Shakespeare walked out of a shadow and stood next to the bed, his golden face glinting in the stage lights.

'I was sent him by a man called Mr Blaze, who owns this mansion. I did not know anything about Mr Blaze, or why he had sent me the toy, so I decided to write a play about him. The story starts in the bedroom of another girl, ten years ago.'

Felix felt a strange sensation as her bed started to move – in fact, the whole stage was moving. It rotated around, taking Felix away from the light.

She got out of the bed and walked across the stage, realising she hadn't thought about doing this. Shakespeare must be controlling her, like a puppet on a string. It felt weird, but there was nothing she could do to stop it. Felix found herself opening a door.

The lights shone on her once again. She was in the set of another bedroom. This one was a similar size but had grander furniture, with a large oak bed at the centre. In the bed was one of the smaller monsters, and two monsters in white coats stood nearby, obviously playing doctors.

'This little girl was called Bindi Blaze and she was ten years old.' Felix found that she no longer needed the script for the play. Shakespeare would make sure she knew Amelie's lines. 'Bindi lived in Murkhill Mansion with her father and had always dreamed of being an actress. Like me, she could not get out of bed, because of severe illness. Her father was a rich inventor of robotic toys, and had paid for the best doctors to look after her. One thing he could not do, though, was buy her happiness.'

Felix moved to one side of the stage as the bedroom door opened and a figure stepped in. Felix could tell it was one of the monsters — it had the same billowing black cloak — but its face had changed. It was an exact copy of Mr Blaze's head from the painting Felix had seen before, his black hair greased back. The face was still a mask, though, its expression concerned but unchanging.

Mr Blaze walked up to the bed and said in a soft, deep voice, 'My dearest Bindi, how are you?'

'I am alright, Daddy, but the doctors scare me when they talk about my illness.'

'They are doing the best they can for you, Bindi.'

'I know. Can I see my friends again soon?'

'Hopefully, when you are stronger.'

Mr Blaze stroked Bindi's face and she smiled up at him.

The bedroom faded into darkness and a beam of light shone on Mr Blaze.

'I am worried about Bindi,' he said to the audience. 'She is being very brave, but I can sense she is scared about what will happen to her. Watching her become sadder and lonelier each day is heartbreaking. I know! I can invent a toy to keep her company. But it cannot just be an ordinary toy. It cannot even be one of the robotic toys I am famous for creating. This toy has to have the power to make Bindi happy, to be her friend and make her dreams come true. I do not have the knowledge to create such a toy, though. I need help.'

The lighting changed and Mr Blaze started to walk across the stage. 'Three months have passed. I have travelled all over the world to find the people who can help me create Bindi's toy. In America, I met a scientist.'

A laboratory was revealed to the left side of the stage, and one of the monsters, dressed in a scientist's lab coat, showed Mr Blaze lots of test tubes full of multicoloured liquids.

'These chemicals are all taken from human blood,'

the scientist explained. 'By combining them with pure gold and heating the mixture to exactly five hundred degrees, you will be able to create a mask capable of understanding human thought.'

The scientist gave the test tubes to Mr Blaze and they shook hands.

'In India, after a month of searching, I discovered a wizard in a cave at the heart of a mountain,' said Mr Blaze.

A spotlight shone on another area of the stage to reveal a monster in golden robes, sitting in front of a small fire. Mr Blaze walked over and sat next to him.

'Here are the claws of the Biwrixle bird,' the wizard croaked, passing them to him with a shaking hand. 'And this is black cloth made of finest byspelt. Combined, they will allow your toy to grant any wish and make dreams come true.'

The spotlight on the wizard faded and more lights revealed a circus tent to the right of the stage, with a monster wearing robes covered in oriental dragon patterns standing next to Mr Blaze.

'After another month of searching, I found a hypnotist in a Chinese circus.'

The hypnotist handed Mr Blaze the small purse. 'The gems in this purse are precious, made of pure mesmerite. When you look at them, they will allow you to forget about your worries and feel happy.'

'These gems will make perfect eyes for Bindi's toy,'

Mr Blaze explained. 'Thank you.' He turned back to the audience. 'I took all my new knowledge and items back to my own laboratory on Thistlewick and began to experiment.'

The set rotated round to show a large, dark room with a long workbench stretched across it and several machines ticking and humming away. On the walls at the back, two monsters were hung up, and Mr Blaze walked over to stand at the workbench and examine and stitch up a third monster.

As he attached the Biwrixle bird's claws to the toy, Mr Blaze said, 'It has now taken me three attempts and six long months to create Bindi's toy. All the while, I have worried that the more time I spend working on this, the less time I get to spend with Bindi. But I know that once this toy is finished, it will make her so happy, and that is more important than anything.'

From the side of the stage, Felix watched Mr Blaze work. She thought about the story she was acting out with the monsters – the story that Amelie believed she had invented. Judging by Amelie's diary, she had never known that Shakespeare was actually capable of making her happy and bringing her imagination to life. And yet everything she had written about in this play – the gems used as the toy's eyes that made you happy when you stared at them, and the wizard's items that meant the toy could grant wishes – seemed to fit with the Shakespeare toy in real life.

Wow! Felix thought. *Maybe this isn't just a story from Amelie's imagination – maybe it's the story of the real Mr Blaze and how he gave Shakespeare his powers.*

After all, Amelie had said she got the idea for the play when she was looking at Shakespeare. He could have made the story appear in her mind.

'Aha!' exclaimed Mr Blaze, lifting up one of the monsters. 'The toy is complete!'

He rushed out of his laboratory. The stage quickly revolved again to show Bindi's bedroom, with the two doctors standing in it.

Mr Blaze entered the room, but Bindi wasn't in her bed. He turned to one of the doctors.

'Where is my daughter?'

'I am ever so sorry, Mr Blaze. I am afraid Bindi died in the night.'

Mr Blaze collapsed to the ground in a devastated heap.

The lights faded out and only Felix could be seen.

She turned to the audience and, speaking as Amelie, said, 'Mr Blaze was heartbroken by the death of his daughter. Not long after her funeral he moved away from Thistlewick, to a house in England, where he became a recluse.'

A brick wall lowered onto the stage from above – the wall of a house. Mr Blaze walked up to the door in the wall, opened it and walked through. He shut it firmly behind him.

'Nine long years passed,' Felix continued. 'Mr Blaze never saw any visitors. He never again invented a toy, so sad was he about his daughter. Then he heard news about my parents and me.'

The door swung open and Mr Blaze stood there, looking excited. 'I have heard of a girl who has been taken seriously ill on Thistlewick. I missed the chance to give Bindi happiness, but now I can make up for that. I will offer this girl's family my mansion and, for her birthday, I will send her a special gift.'

The lights faded out and, as the stage revolved once more, Felix found herself walking back to the middle of it. In the dark, she climbed under the soft duvet on Amelie's bed.

'It was my tenth birthday when I received Mr Blaze's present, the rag toy that I named Shakespeare.' She raised her arm up to point at Shakespeare, who was once again standing next to her bed. 'Mr Blaze's note with the toy said, "I hope this helps you to make your dreams come true." I thought about my dreams, and what I wanted to wish for. I could wish to go climbing or sailing, or on some other adventure, but those kinds of things didn't seem important. I laid in my bed and thought for days about what my most important wish was. Then I got it.'

She turned to face Shakespeare and his golden, happy face stared down at her.

'Shakespeare, my wish is this: when I die, I want my parents to be happy. I do not want them to become sad and lonely like Mr Blaze. Can you make that happen?'

Shakespeare smiled at her. A golden glow surrounded him and his head slowly tilted up and down. Then he pointed towards Amelie's bedroom door. It opened and two monsters walked in, both with golden, happy faces. One was wearing a green cardigan, the other a long, flowing dress. They walked up to the bed and hugged their daughter.

'We love you so much, Amelie.'

'Mum, Dad, I love you too!' said Felix.

She turned to the audience. Although the lights shining on her were bright, she could just make out the front row of the audience below her. Their eyes were fixed on her – they were all gripped by Amelie's story.

'And as my parents hugged me, I knew that Shakespeare would make my wish come true. I knew that even when I died, my parents would always be happy.'

The lights started to slowly fade and, as they did, Felix smiled at the audience as warmly as she could manage.

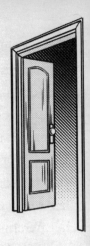

23

Amelie's Most
Important Wish

The ten monsters, their faces all now a fixed golden smile, walked towards the front of the stage and Felix joined them, moving into the gap they had left for her in the centre.

The lights came up and the audience clapped loudly. Felix saw her mum beaming at her, and Mayor Merryweather with a big grin stretched across his moustache. Were they genuinely happy, or were they being hypnotised by Shakespeare's mesmerite eyes?

Then Felix did a double take, for in between them, in the seat that had previously been the only empty one in the whole theatre, she noticed a girl.

Amelie Summercroft's eyes were far brighter than Felix had imagined. Sitting in her nightdress, Amelie's brown hair was pushed back from her freckly face and she was smiling happily.

Felix wasn't sure if Amelie was really there or just in her imagination. She watched as the little girl slowly and peacefully faded away, like smoke after a fire.

As the curtains closed and the audience's clapping died down, Felix felt a strange mixture of emotions. She felt happy for Amelie, knowing that she had helped to make her second biggest wish come true. But she also felt so sorry for her. Amelie was trapped in bed, fifty years in the past, without her mum and dad. How could her most important wish ever come true in real life if her parents weren't there?

Felix wheeled round to the monsters. 'Right, I have brought the whole of Thistlewick to watch Amelie's play. I have performed in it with you. Now, you have to return everything to normal. Give me back Drift and Caspar, release everyone else you've captured, and give Amelie back her parents!'

The monsters all stood in a line and fixed their faces on Felix.

She went to the bed and grabbed Amelie's diary. She held it out to Shakespeare.

'Read it. Fifty years ago when Amelie wrote this diary, she was trapped in bed, not knowing how long she had left to live, and she didn't have her parents because *you* took them away from her. Amelie's play being performed was only her second biggest wish. You heard what her most important wish was in the play.' She looked desperately at Shakespeare, unsure if he was even able to change the monsters back into normal people. She just had to hope he could!

Felix tried a different approach. 'The story in the play was true, wasn't it? Mr Blaze created you for his daughter, Bindi, but she died and he became a recluse. Then he sent you to make Amelie's wishes come true?'

Shakespeare nodded his head and, as one, the other monsters tilted their heads up and down too.

'Then you have failed. There is no way you can make Amelie's most important wish come true, unless you give her parents back to her.'

The monsters stared at Felix again. Long, fixed stares. Her heart thumping, she started to back away, sure that their faces were about to glow red, that they were going to attack her, to turn her into one of them. Had she failed, after everything?

But then, as one, they tilted their heads up and down. Up and down.

Felix watched them with growing confidence.

The heads kept moving up and down, faster and faster. A golden glow formed around the monsters' bodies as their heads moved faster still. Felix's mouth opened wide as the two monsters in the middle – Romeo and Juliet – rocketed upwards, their cloaks a blur of black as they disappeared out of sight.

In their place stood a man and a woman.

The man wore glasses and a green cardigan, and the woman a long, flowing dress. Felix recognised them from the photo in the library. Amelie's parents. Felix let her mouth form a smile as she took the sight of them in.

'Thank you,' said Amelie's mum.

'For giving us the chance to see our daughter again,' said Amelie's dad.

They both faded away, just like Amelie had. Felix hoped they were heading back fifty years, to their daughter trapped in her bedroom.

The heads of the other monsters were still vibrating, their bodies glowing gold.

Two more – Hamlet and Ophelia – shot into the air, revealing a girl in pigtails and a friendly looking young man in a white coat.

'You must be Elfie and Dr Ralph,' said Felix.

The man winked at her and the girl smiled.

'Elfie, you need to get Amelie's old classmates to go and see her. She misses you all, even Bartley.'

Elfie nodded and they both faded into nothing.

Three more monsters soared away in quick succession, allowing two men and a woman to fade back to where they had come from.

Three monsters were left. Shakespeare, Titania and Oberon.

'Come on, Drift and Caspar!' Felix said, desperate to get her friends back.

But nothing happened. Felix's smile started to fade. The monsters just stood there, their heads shaking.

'What … what do I have to do to get them back, Shakespeare? Tell me!'

The monsters fell motionless, their heads hung low.

Felix took a step towards them, starting to panic. Why wasn't Shakespeare letting Caspar and Drift go?

Shakespeare, standing in the centre, lifted his head up. He raised an arm and pointed a claw at Felix, then slowly over to the bed.

'You want me to get into the bed again?'

Shakespeare shook his head and pointed from Felix to the bed again.

She looked at the diary in her hand, now with only three scratches, and understood. She took the diary back over to the bed and placed it gently down on Amelie's pillow.

A loud bang made her jump. She turned to watch one of the monsters explode like a firework, quickly followed by another.

They left behind them two figures, one stood up, the other sprawled on the ground.

'Drift!' Felix cried. 'Caspar!'

She had never been so happy to see them. She ran forwards and hugged Drift. Then she helped Caspar up and hugged him too.

'I thought I'd lost you.'

'Thank you, Felix!'

'You saved us,' said Drift. 'I am never ever playing a board game again.'

'But what about Shakespeare? What will happen to him?' asked Caspar, pointing to the monster, whose head was now moving up and down so fast it was a blur.

'I don't know,' said Felix.

Shakespeare suddenly stopped vibrating. He floated gently up into the air and looked down at Felix with a golden, happy smile. Then, using his cloak as wings, he flew away and up through the ceiling.

Felix stared at the ground, but nothing stood there to replace the monster.

'Maybe he has become a rag toy again, up in Amelie's room.' She looked at her friends. 'Are you both OK?'

Caspar nodded.

'It was weird being trapped like that,' said Drift. 'Really weird.'

'Did you know what was going on?'

'Yes,' said Caspar. 'Sort of. The monsters attached themselves onto us and took over our minds and our bodies.'

'But we were still in there, watching everything that was happening – just unable to do anything,' said Drift.

'Come on,' said Felix. 'Let's get you two out of here.'

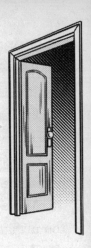

24

A Different Future

Felix, Caspar and Drift walked out of the theatre. The library was empty, but they heard lots of chatter nearby. They strode into the entrance hall and were greeted by cheers.

Everyone seemed to be there. Their parents, Mayor Merryweather, and even the workers had come in to cheer them.

Felix felt herself being patted on the shoulder as she walked through the islanders.

'Impressive, very impressive,' said Mr Potts.

'A triumph,' said Mrs Turner.

'Weren't those masks you used wonderful?' said Mrs Didsbury. 'Full of expression.'

Felix tried to head towards her mum, who was smiling at her, but she got stopped by Mr Finch, who asked how all the scene changes had worked. Then more islanders piled in and started quizzing them about the play.

All the while, Felix couldn't get Amelie out of her

mind. What had happened – had her parents returned to her? Felix had to find out.

She managed to slip away from the crowd of people, leaving Caspar and Drift to answer their questions. She walked over to the marble staircase, passing the eagle, now once more made of solid, unmoving stone. She climbed the stairs.

At the top she found a door and opened it. Inside was the living room with the old-fashioned TV. She closed the door and opened it again. Still the living room. So the mansion must have returned to normal. She felt her body relax for the first time in two days.

Felix knew exactly where she wanted to go. Along a corridor she found another flight of stairs. At the top of them was a hallway with several doors leading off it. On the white door at the end was a sign with a border of flowers: 'Amelie's room'.

Holding her breath, Felix twisted the handle and opened the door.

It really did feel like she had been in this room before, it was so similar to the set on the stage. The bed sheets were a different flowery pattern, there were no machines and a few different items were placed around the room, but otherwise it was the same.

Felix went straight over to the bed. At the end of it she found a small rag toy. It was about twenty centimetres tall, with a long black cloak and a golden, smiley face.

'Hello, Shakespeare.'

But as she stared at him, she didn't feel overly happy and she didn't forget about her worries. He wasn't hypnotising her.

'You're just a normal toy now, aren't you?'

Next to Shakespeare was Amelie's diary. Felix picked it up. There were no scratches now. She flicked through it and found the last entry she had read, dated July 8th 1965, the one where Amelie had wished her play could be performed and that her parents would return. Felix turned the page and her eyes grew wide. There was now another diary entry after it, dated July 9th. She eagerly started reading.

Dear diary,

I didn't have a nightmare last night. I had a dream. The most realistic and enjoyable dream I have had for a long time.

In the dream, I was sitting in a theatre, just like the one I drew, watching my play being performed. The theatre was full of other people – at least 300, I guessed. Another girl was performing as me. She didn't look anything like me – she had a ponytail and was wearing a T-shirt and trousers, the kind a boy would wear. But she acted really well. At the end everyone clapped loudly. I was very happy that they had enjoyed the play.

It was only a dream, I know, but it made me feel great.

When I opened my eyes life instantly got a million times better. Mum and Dad stood at the foot of my bed. I was so glad to see them! I leapt up and knocked one of the machines over! Dad put it back upright again, then they both hugged me tightly.

'Dad, I've solved that riddle about the two knights in front of the two doors,' I said.

He was very impressed that I got the right answer. I told him I was going to write it down in here, but he thought I shouldn't. He said that someone might read this diary one day and they might want to try and solve it themselves.

Well, have you worked out the answer? I hope so. It's really obvious, when you think of it!

'I did manage to, Amelie,' said Felix, a large smile stretched across her face. 'Well, Caspar did, anyway.'

She was so relieved and happy for Amelie that she felt like jumping up and down.

There were no other diary entries after that. Maybe Amelie hadn't needed her diary once she got her parents back. Felix still wanted to know what happened to Amelie, though, and whether her most important wish had come true.

There was a collection of black and white photos on a dressing table under the window. Felix walked over and studied them closely.

One was of Amelie in a wheelchair, her eyes bright,

her parents standing behind her, down on the beach. They certainly all looked happy. Another photo showed Amelie with Dr Ralph, pulling silly faces at the camera. The next photo made Felix's heart skip. In the centre was Amelie; next to her stood Elfie and around them were their nine other classmates. It was easy to spot Bartley – the one with a scowl.

'Lovely, isn't it?' a voice came from the door.

Felix turned and saw an old man standing there. He was stooped over a walking stick and had a thin crop of grey hair.

'Yes,' she replied, wondering who the man was. 'Do you know what happened to Amelie after these photos were taken?'

'I do. She lived a short but incredibly happy life, for two more years.'

'Oh, so she…' Felix's voice trailed off and she felt tears welling in her eyes.

The man added, 'It was far longer than any of the doctors had predicted she would hold on for – even me.'

'What was it that made her so ill?' Felix asked.

'Amelie had cancer, though she never liked to talk about it. And back in those days, we weren't able to treat it like they do now.'

'You said, "even me" – are you a doctor?'

The old man walked slowly over to her and suddenly Felix knew who he was. He had aged a lot in the last fifty years, but she recognised his face.

'You're Dr Ralph!'

'Yes, Felix, I am.'

'Do you remember what happened in the theatre, when we performed Amelie's play?'

'I do. That moment when I faded away, I was taken fifty years back in time to when I had entered Murkhill Mansion on 3rd July 1965. But for you it must have only just happened.'

Felix nodded. 'I guess the theatre doesn't exist any more, now that Shakespeare has returned the mansion to normal.'

'That theatre doesn't exist, no. However, Amelie's parents did build her a theatre, inside Murkhill Mansion, based on her drawings.' With a shaking hand, Dr Ralph picked up the photo of Amelie and her classmates. 'Amelie was even well enough at one point to perform her play in the theatre, with her friends helping. Everyone on Thistlewick came to watch. It was a truly special occasion.'

Felix felt tears in her eyes again, but for a different reason now. She had an overwhelming sense of joy for Amelie.

Then she frowned. 'Is Murkhill Mansion still going to be demolished?'

Dr Ralph smiled. 'No. When Amelie's parents came back, the future changed. They no longer disappeared in mysterious circumstances, and lived in Murkhill Mansion long after Amelie's death.'

'And did Amelie's most important wish come true? Were her parents happy after she died?'

Dr Ralph smiled. 'They were deeply sad for a while, of course. But they remembered how happy Amelie had been in her last few months and eventually that made them happy. Each year they put on plays in Amelie's theatre and the whole of Thistlewick came together to celebrate her life. When her parents died a few years ago, Murkhill Mansion was donated to the Thistlewick council, to be used as Thistlewick's theatre. We still put on lots of plays here.'

'Oh, I'm so glad!'

Dr Ralph waved his stick at the door and Felix joined him in walking back out.

They strolled along the corridor in silence. When they got to the top of the marble stairs that led down to the entrance hall, the place was empty, except for Caspar and Drift.

They looked up at Felix and waved.

'Everyone went home very quickly,' she said. 'Or … wait. Everything that just happened – the bulldozers and me performing Amelie's play with the monsters – did that now never happen?'

'Correct,' replied Dr Ralph. 'In this new future it didn't happen, because it never needed to happen.'

'But you still remember it?'

'The only people who will remember what went on – exactly how you saved us and made Amelie's wishes come true – are you, your two friends, and everyone else who was turned into those monsters.'

Felix smiled, and decided she quite liked that. It was their secret.

She helped Dr Ralph make his way slowly down the stairs. When they reached the bottom, Caspar and Drift came over to join them.

'Dr Ralph, meet Caspar and Drift,' said Felix. 'They probably look a bit different from the last time you saw them.'

Dr Ralph held out a hand and the boys both shook it.

'On behalf of all of us who were trapped, and especially Amelie, I would like to say the biggest of thank yous to you all.' Dr Ralph beamed at them. 'Now, I really must show you Amelie's theatre. Then, if you don't mind, I have a new juggling act I would like to try out on you. I may look ancient, but there's still a surprising amount of energy in old Dr Ralph.'

The four of them made their way towards the library door. As they went, Dr Ralph crossed his eyes and pulled a silly face at Felix, making her burst out laughing. Her laughter rang around the entrance hall and sounded just like the cry of a golden eagle.

Felix looked up at the empty ceiling and grinned.

'Watch out for falling tortoises,' she said.

Felix's other exciting adventures:

Book 1:

Felix finds out that her evil head teacher, Mr Foxsworth, is looking for treasure. Hundred of years ago the treasure belonged to a bloodthirsty pirate, Captain Traiton. Can Felix get to the treasure before Mr Foxsworth, and what will happen when the past and the present collide?

Book 3:

A mysterious ship appears off the coast of Thistlewick. On board is a dark, creepy woman, and a man who wants revenge on Felix and will destroy the whole of Thistlewick to get it.

Can Felix figure out how to stop their evil plans before it's too late?

www.luketemple.co.uk